PICKING PISMO

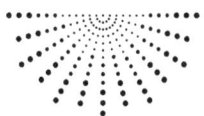

EMI HILTON

Copyright © 2024 by Emi Hilton, PICKING PISMO

All rights reserved.

This is a fictional work. The names, characters, incidents, and locations are solely the concepts and products of the author's imagination, or are used to create a fictitious story and should not be construed as real. No part of this book may be reproduced in any form or by any electronic or mechanical means, including information storage and retrieval systems, without written permission from the author, except for the use of brief quotations in a book review.

Published by 5 PRINCE PUBLISHING & BOOKS, LLC

PO Box 865, Arvada, CO 80001

www.5PrinceBooks.com

ISBN digital: 978-1-63112-378-8

ISBN print: 978-1-63112-382-5

Cover Credit: Marianne Nowicki

F072324

*To my Schofield family and
all the beautiful memories
we share together
in Pismo Beach.*

ACKNOWLEDGMENTS

First, I would like to thank my readers. Thank you for following me on my writing journey, purchasing my books, sharing with a friend, and leaving five-star reviews. You are helping me live out my dream. A million thanks.

Second, I thank my publisher, 5 Prince Books. Thank you for believing in me and helping make all my writer dreams come true. From the deepest part of my heart, I am beyond grateful my stories have found a home at your publishing house.

Next, I thank my editor, Cate Byers. It was a pleasure working with you a second time. Once again, you are a pure delight. Thank you for being my champion. I appreciate your patience with me as I grow as a writer.

As always, I am nothing without my other half, my husband Tyler. I love you beyond words. Our love is what inspires me to write.

To my family and friends, thank you for your kind words, support and encouragement. I am truly blessed to have every single one of you in my life.

Last, I thank my faithful Father in Heaven. I thank thee for walking beside me and guiding me. I thank thee for giving me the words to write. I know everything is possible with thee. I will praise thy holy name all the days of my life. I humbly devote the glory and honor to thee.

ALSO BY EMI HILTON

Leaving Cloverton

Picking Pismo

PICKING PISMO

CHAPTER ONE

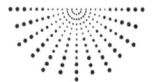

"So, any idea of when you'll get your braces off?" asked Claire as she drove through the pint-sized town of Pismo Beach.

The familiar shops of Claire's childhood faded into a sea of colors through her back window. Glancing in her rearview mirror, Claire caught Alexis's shrug.

Throwing up a hand, Claire continued, "Take a wild guess."

"How would I know?" hissed Alexis. Narrowing her eyes into tiny slits, Alexis flashed a directed glare. The car pulsed with catastrophic energy, almost combustible. "I'm *only* thirteen." After a dramatic eye roll, Alexis dropped her head back down, burying her attention once again in her phone screen.

"I know you're only thirteen." Claire forced her voice to be even, refusing to let a thirteen-year-old rattle her. Though during the recent days, it proved to be incredibly difficult. "But, I figured maybe the orthodontist mentioned it to you at your other appointments."

"No," said Alexis in a vague whisper. Alexis peered out the

passenger side window, pausing. Running a finger across the glass, she continued, "Mom always talked to Dr. Clark at the end."

Whoosh. *Mom.* Claire's heart clenched tight, and the air became stifling. Tugging at the collar of her shirt, Claire attempted to rid her skin of the restriction of her clothing. Eyes itching, she rubbed them to keep the tears at bay. Oh, how she wished Mom was still here. She'd know how to handle Alexis, and her full-blown teenage fury.

Honestly, the two sisters were practically strangers. Claire had left for college before Alexis even started grade school. When Claire came home to visit for the holidays, she usually took Alexis for ice cream, or maybe a trip to the park. Then after a few days, Claire would return to Los Angeles to her real life, job, and friends. She now regretted not visiting more over the past few years, but hindsight was always 20/20.

Silence enveloped the car, only widening the distance between the two sisters. Biting on the inside of her cheek, Claire paused. If she misspoke, the headway she had gained over the last weeks with Alexis might take a major step back. Alexis was grieving, tiptoeing her way through the various stages of the grief cycle, coming to grips with her life never being the same without Mom in it. Sympathy wiggled its way into her heart. Alexis wasn't a bad kid, and Claire needed to recognize how grief sometimes manifested itself as anger.

With a loud wistful sigh, Alexis said, "I wish Mom was here..." Her voice faded away. Then—almost as if a planned attack—her jaw locked, and eyes narrowed. "Not you," Alexis hissed.

Claire flinched. Blinking rapidly, she forced away the emotions bubbling to the surface. *Don't cry. Don't cry. Don't. Cry. This isn't about you, not directly. She misses Mom.* Even though the insult was tangled up in grief, it still stung.

Pushing her hair over her shoulder, Claire blew out a long rattling breath. "I know," whispered Claire. After making a left into the parking lot of the orthodontist's office, Claire continued louder, "Me too, kid. Me too. I miss Mom every day. I wish she was here too." Her shoulders drooped and chest pinched tighter.

Finding an empty spot, Claire parked. Immediately, Alexis jumped out of the car before Claire even turned off the engine. Alexis wandered into Dr Clark's office, leaving Claire alone in the car. Claire slumped in her seat, trying to not let the feeling of defeat overtake her.

Staring out the window at the orthodontist's office, Claire wondered if parents went inside and waited. Or did she tell Alexis to text her when she was done? Pondering her predicament for a few moments, Claire climbed out of the car, walking to the front door.

Claire needed to speak to the office about the payment of Alexis's braces. Nowhere in any of Mom's financial records did she find a remaining balance. Keeping her fingers crossed, Claire hoped Mom had already paid for the braces in full. Alexis's finances were tight enough, and Claire didn't think she could afford another payment if it was required. Maybe she could charge it? But then how would she ever pay it off? Their expenses seemed to be a never-ending list. Kids were *so* expensive.

When Claire received the news of Mom's sudden passing, she took a three-month sabbatical from her physical therapy job in Los Angeles. Three months of unpaid time off. Three months to pack up her sister and all their stuff, sell Mom's home, and bring Alexis back with her to Los Angeles. Apparently, years ago, Mom took a second out on the mortgage. Claire didn't have a choice, as much as it pained her, she needed to sell her childhood home to break even. Fast.

Alexis was furious about the plan, because her friends and life were in Pismo Beach. Many sleepless nights, Claire went over and over her budget. As much as she didn't want to uproot Alexis, financially, it wasn't possible to stay. The landlord of her apartment in Los Angeles refused to release her from the terms of their lease agreement, even after Claire explained the situation. So, she'd let Alexis finish the school year, then they'd return to Los Angeles and try to build some semblance of a new life.

Pushing open the door to the orthodontist's office, the door chimed as Claire entered. Glancing around the small waiting room, Claire didn't spot Alexis, so she peeked into the large communal exam room with a long row of dental chairs. Locating Alexis reclined in a chair with a dental assistant already adjusting her braces, Claire walked over to the reception desk.

A woman in her mid to late forties with curly brown hair sat behind the reception desk. She glanced up from her computer screen at Claire's arrival.

"Good morning, I'm Sarah," said Sarah brightly. Her eyes sparkled kindly back at Claire. "How may I help you today?"

Leaning forward on the reception counter, Claire fiddled with the cup of pens next to the sign in sheet. "Good morning, Sarah." She bit her bottom lip. Claire continued, "My sister Alexis is here getting her braces adjusted." She let go of the pens and stood straight, adjusting her slipping purse strap.

Interrupting her, Sarah wagged a finger at her. "I thought there was a resemblance. Sisters? What are you like double her age?" Sarah scooted backward on her rolling chair, grabbing a file from the wall-to-wall shelving behind her. She swiveled back to face her, flipping through the file without looking up.

Claire tucked some flyaway hair behind her ears. "You almost guessed right, we're fourteen years apart."

People were always amazed at the age gap between Claire and Alexis, especially with no other siblings in between. Alexis was a surprise. The day Mom told Dad she was pregnant; he took off and never came back. Dad never wanted children, so two kids was out of the question.

"Anyways," Claire shuffled her feet. "I needed to find out how much of a balance is remaining for my sister's braces."

Glancing up, Sarah tilted her head to the side. "I'm sorry." Sarah shut the file in her hands and tossed it into a bin. "I can't discuss that information with you since you aren't on the account. Is your mom here?" Sarah glanced past Claire, surveying the waiting room. When Sarah didn't spot Mom, she reverted her gaze back to Claire.

Claire took a deep settling breath, bracing herself. "Our mom passed away, suddenly, a month ago. I'm now Alexis's legal guardian, so…" A pinch between her shoulder blades made her neck stiffen. "Could you let me know how much we still owe?"

Sarah's eyes widened, awkwardly, she shifted in her seat. "That's so tragic. I mean how…" She waved a hand, looking away. Moving the mouse around, her computer screen lit back up. With a few more clicks of her mouse, Claire guessed Sarah was searching for Alexis's account information. She stopped clicking and met Claire's gaze. "I'm really sorry for your loss."

"Thanks." Claire didn't want to elaborate. If she did, then the tears started, and sometimes, they didn't stop for a long time. "So, about that balance." Leaning over the reception counter again, Claire gazed at Sarah's computer screen.

Holding up a single finger, Sarah said, "Let me go check with Dr. Clark." Abruptly, Sarah stood. "I'll be right back." She wandered into the exam room filled with dental chairs.

When Sarah didn't return immediately, Claire opted to sit down and wait. Every inch of the coffee table was covered with random magazines. Mindlessly, she selected a magazine on top to occupy herself. Flipping through the home reno magazine, she closely examined a before and after photo.

"Are you Alexis's sister?" a man's voice out of nowhere asked.

Startled, Claire dropped the magazine right out of her hands. Bending down to pick it up, Claire slowly took in the darked haired man with dimples. He wore scrubs with a white lab coat over them. Unconsciously, Claire smoothed out her own dark brown hair thrown up into an untamable bun. If Claire knew Alexis's orthodontist's office had hotties walking around, she'd at least have combed her hair. Wondering if she had lip gloss on, Claire almost moved her hand to her lips to double check, but she stopped herself in time.

"Yes. I'm Claire." Tossing the magazine back onto the coffee table, Claire stood. She even remembered to straighten her shoulders.

He offered a hand. "I'm Dr. Clark." A smile spread across his face, making her middle do a weird flip-turn. "Alexis's orthodontist. It's nice to meet you." His blue eyes dazzled back at her.

Zero chance this guy was single. Claire wanted to do a ring check, but she forced herself to keep her eyes on his face. "Likewise. I'm Claire..." she stammered then waved a hand. "I mean I already told you that."

Fiddling with her purse strap, Claire waited for him to continue the conversation. She clearly forgot how to speak normally.

Dr. Clark glanced over his shoulder toward Sarah. Claire caught the look they exchanged with one another. He wrung his hands together, shifting back to Claire. "I understand you lost your mom recently."

"Yes," Claire paused, glancing in the direction of Sarah. "I did. I mean, we did, Alexis and I."

Sarah shrank into herself, darting her gaze away and to her computer screen. Quickly, she moved her mouse around and started typing.

"I'm very sorry for your loss," said Dr. Clark. "Sarah said you were asking about the remaining balance for your sister's braces?"

Claire managed a nod.

"Please, don't worry about what you owe." Dr. Clark waved a hand. "I'd like to drop the remaining balance."

"Oh..." Her gaze darted between Sarah and Dr. Clark. Claire glanced at her feet then back at him. "I mean, I can't let you do that. Just tell me the amount, and I'll figure something out."

A trickle of sweat dripped down her temple. Why was she sweating so much? It wasn't even hot.

"No. I insist." Dr. Clark's gaze skidded across her face. The worry lines on his brow deepened. Lowering his voice, he continued, "I read what happened in the newspaper. I'm sorry. It's all so... tragic. It's the least I can do to help."

Claire sucked in the air. Her temples rang, while sweat pooled at the small of her back. So, he saw the article in the newspaper and made the connection. In a small town, nothing remained private. Even the parts of life you didn't want to share.

For the past month, Claire desperately tried to make sense of everything. Losing Mom, wrapping her head around mortality. One minute you're living your life, then bam everything crashes down on you. Mom, her bedrock, her solid foundation, was gone.

With shaky hands, Claire forced them into the pockets of

her jeans. Her eyes burned, a lump forming in her throat. "Thank you then…" Her voice cracked. She averted her gaze, unable to look Dr. Clark in the eye for one more second. The emotions within her danced too close to the surface, trying to break free. Four weeks in, Claire found ways to push them back down. Exhaling, she pleaded with herself to hold it together and not lose it in an orthodontist's office, with a kind and unassuming man. "We appreciate it."

Dr. Clark gave a small nod. "Okay then, I'm finishing up with Alexis." His lips formed a crooked tight smile. "I'll come get you when she's ready." Then he left, returning to the exam room with its half a dozen dental chairs.

Stunned, Claire stumbled back a few steps until she found her seat again. Slumping into a seat, she practiced her breathing method she learned in yoga. Mindlessly, she counted, waiting until her rapid heartrate returned to normal. Eventually, the tremor in her hands subsided too. She managed to remove her hands from her pockets and tightly grip them together on her lap.

A few other patients came and went, giving Claire time to move her thoughts from grief to the kindness of strangers. If she learned anything through this experience, there was no shortage of goodness. Even with the unspeakable bad, the good far outweighed it. Goodness prevailed, and her little community in Pismo Beach overwhelmed her with their generosity. She whispered a silent prayer. Deep in thought, someone calling her name, broke her trance.

"Claire," Dr. Clark appeared in the threshold between the waiting room and exam room.

"Yes," Claire stumbled to her feet, eventually finding her footing.

"Why don't you follow me back?" Dr. Clark motioned for her to follow him. "Alexis's adjustment is completed."

Claire wandered behind Dr. Clark into the communal

exam room. Alexis was reclined in one of the dental chairs. Dr. Clark sat down on the swivel stool next to her. Grabbing some gloves off the side table, Dr. Clark put them on. Claire remained standing on the other side of Alexis.

Dr. Clark asked Alexis to open her mouth, and Alexis complied.

With his hands in her mouth, Dr. Clark pointed to a few teeth. "I wanted to show you the progress."

Taking a step closer, Claire leaned in to get a better view of Alexis's mouth. Her nostrils flared, catching a whiff of his cologne. Mind elsewhere, Claire didn't listen as Dr. Clark pointed and prodded at her sister's mouth. Claire wondered how long it took him to get his perfect five o'clock shadow. When Dr. Clark paused, looking over at her, Claire realized her error.

Her cheeks flushed with heat. Claire scratched her head. "Could you repeat that last part?"

"I said," Dr. Clark turned off the overhead light, pushing it back to its proper place. "She's on track to get her braces off in six months." Then he instructed Alexis to sit up, stripping his gloves off, revealing his bare ring finger. He tossed his gloves into the trash.

"Six months!" squealed Claire. Realizing her overreaction, Claire cleared her throat and tucked some unruly hair behind her ears. "I mean, is it possible she could get them off sooner?"

Claire didn't have six months.

Dr. Clark stood, grabbing Alexis's medical chart off the side table next to the dental chair. He shook his head. "I don't see that happening." Flipping through her chart, Dr. Clark double-checked the photos attached to the back. Then he snapped the file shut. "It's like I showed you, there's still too much movement that needs to happen before Alexis can get them off."

Claire pinched the bridge of her nose, forcing herself to calm down. "We have to be out of Mom's house in ninety days." She gnawed on the inside of her cheeks. "Scratch that, like seventy-six days. I don't…" She threw her hands down at her side, trying her best to not spiral into a ball of stress.

It was like she was on a child's teeter-totter. Up and down. All day long. The smallest thing pushed her almost to a breaking point, things months prior, she would've taken in stride.

"Hey," Dr. Clark's voice was warm and steady, loosening the knot forming in her belly. He tilted his head to the side. "Let's not worry about any of that right now. Okay?" His gaze skidded across her face, making her heart palpitate.

Hypnotically, Claire repeated, "Okay." Her uptick of stress dissipated. "I'll worry about it later," she robotically stated.

Alexis grumbled, "Can we go already?" Her gaze flicked between Claire and Dr. Clark.

Claire paused, blinking. "Yes, of course." Digging into her purse, she located her keys. "If you want, you can go wait in the car while we finish up." She held them out to Alexis.

Snatching the keys from Claire's hands Alexis said, "Fine." Then Alexis brushed past Claire, nearly making Claire stumble forward.

With the chart in his hands, Dr. Clark stood too.

Once Alexis was out of ear shot, Claire said, "Thanks again for covering the rest of Alexis's braces." She shuffled her feet, moving toward the exit.

"My pleasure." His eyes crinkled around the edges. "I'm sorry for what you and Alexis are going through. I can't imagine." His voice faded off, and Dr. Clark looked away.

This was the part she hated. Claire didn't know how to put others at ease, and Mom's passing was like a dark cloud of gloom wherever she traveled. Instead of acknowledging his comment, Claire decided to pass it right on by. "So, do I just talk to Sarah to schedule Alexis's next appointment?"

"Yep," Dr. Clark placed the file in a box on a side table then started toward a patient waiting in another nearby dental chair. "We'll see both of you in four weeks." Then Dr. Clark sat down on a swivel chair two patients over and started speaking to the patient.

Claire left, wandering to the front reception. She made the appropriate appointment with Sarah and left. After walking to her car, Claire slid into the driver's seat. With her earbuds firmly planted in her ears, Alexis didn't acknowledge her entrance.

"You didn't tell me," Claire started the engine, "your orthodontist was a total hottie."

Alexis removed one earbud. "What?"

Claire repeated, "Dr. Clark is totally hot."

"Gag me." Alexis rolled her eyes and made a gagging motion. "He's like super old. Gross."

"He's not that old." Claire glanced over her shoulder before backing out of her parking space. Then she slowly merged onto the street. "We're probably only a few years apart."

"Exactly," Alexis scoffed. "He's old."

Claire refused to let Alexis get under her skin. She forced a laugh. "Then that means I'm old too."

"Like I said…" Alexis shifted, staring out her passenger side window. "You're old." A long pause, then Alexis caught Claire's glance in the rear-view mirror. "How am I going to get my braces off if we're moving before then?"

"We'll figure something out." Claire gripped the steering wheel. Her endless list of things to do before getting Mom's house on the market rattled off in her head. "We'll drive back down if we have to, because Dr. Clark isn't making us pay the remaining balance on your braces, which is very kind of him."

"Everyone feels bad for us." Alexis shook her head, popping her earbud back into her ear. "And they should… our lives suck. Our Mom's dead. You're stuck with me. And we have no parents and no money."

Karate chop to the gut, Alexis's words knocked the wind out of Claire.

"I— I—" stammered Claire. The world came crashing down on her again, a whirling mess of tragedy. The past weeks of her life were ones Claire never wanted to relive. No doubt she had made a thousand mistakes as she dealt with her mom's affairs and taken on the role as Alexis's pseudo mother. She gazed to her right, taking in the view of the ocean, wishing for its calming presence to dissipate the tension in her chest. "I'm glad we have each other, and I'm sure things will get better with time… for the both of us."

Even the words fell flat to her. Who was she kidding? Things were bleak. Both sisters thrown together due to horrible circumstances. A familiar weight landed on her shoulders, the burden too heavy to carry on her own. Claire paused and whispered a silent prayer.

Alexis interrupted her. "See you don't even believe it. Don't lie to me. I see the train wreck coming. I wish I knew how good I had it before…" She fiddled with her cell phone in her hands.

Claire glanced at the rear-view mirror, catching the sight of tears cascading down Alexis's cheeks. Her throat grew tight. "I wish I had known too," Claire quietly replied.

Silence.

Then Claire added, "Things will improve." Her voice was a tad too cheerful. "Promise."

Swiping the tears away, Alexis pointed to her ear. "I can't

hear you." Then she turned up her music, loud enough Claire heard it seeping out of her earbuds.

Letting out a long, raspy breath, Claire took the long way home. Getting a full view of the ocean, she opened the windows a bit to let the tangy saltwater whirl around her car. Reminders of summers with Mom and Alexis whizzed through her as she remembered sunburns, saltwater taffy, and clam chowder. Her heart ached so much, she found it hard to breathe. Maybe Alexis was right? What if things never improved? Perhaps this burden would forever be too heavy to bear?

Give it to Him.

Claire paused, pushing back at the wave of overwhelming sadness engulfing her. "God, it's yours," Claire stated out loud. "It's all yours."

The words drifted out the window, carried away with the ocean breeze. Claire took another glance at the beautiful ocean, and for a second, the gut-wrenching pain subsided.

CHAPTER TWO

"Mom, are you home?" David walked through his parents' front door, wandering to the back of his childhood home. Jasper, his parents' yorkie greeted him. Bending down, David stroked Jasper between his ears. "Where are they, boy?" he asked.

Jasper barked. David scooped him up and continued out to the patio. Pushing open the sliding glass door, David stared out at the Pacific Ocean in all its splendid glory. He sighed with relief as the sticky saltwater hit his skin. This, the view of the ocean, the healing balm of an ocean breeze, never became old.

His parents were seated at the patio table. They both glanced up as he passed through the sliding door, closing it behind him.

"Here you both are," declared David.

David slung himself into one of the empty patio chairs, setting Jasper down on the ground to wander around. Stephen, his dad, glanced up from his e-book, removing his reading glasses, he placed them on the patio dining table.

Stretching, Stephen said with a chuckle, "We weren't hiding."

"Just enjoying the last little bit of sunshine before the sunset." Kelly, his mom, continued to knit. Her needles moved in tandem across the yellow yarn. She paused when she finished the long row of loops. "This is a nice, pleasant surprise. You usually don't drop by on a Friday night. What's up?"

Grabbing a handful of popcorn from the bowl on the patio table, David popped some into his mouth. Ignoring his mom's digging, David knew Kelly was itching to ask about the woman he took out a few weeks in a row. But it fizzled and burned out about a month ago, and David didn't want to rehash it. Since his divorce, his parents managed to stay out of his dating life. Even if they wanted the details, they didn't ask and only listened when he offered information freely. David appreciated it.

"If I had a view like this, I'd be out here every night too," said David.

Kelly smiled, peering over the top of her glasses. "Someday, dear." She pulled the yarn to give it some more length before starting on the next row of tight loops. "You'll get your big house on the water too."

"Doubtful," leaning back, David crossed his ankles and cradled his neck. The terms of his divorce ran through his head. His jaw tightened. Trying not to think about everything he'd lost, David cranked his neck back and forth. He swallowed, forcing the sting of the past away. Enough. He paused, "Mom, remember that friend of yours who passed away a few weeks ago, the one in your knitting circle?"

"Rebecca?" Kelly stopped mid-knit, peering over.

David snapped then pointed. "Yes, Rebecca. Her daughters came in today. The younger one, Alexis, is a patient of mine."

A hand flew to Kelly's heart. "No, those poor girls. I remember Rebecca mentioning there was quite an age gap between the two of them."

"Uh huh," David grabbed another handful of popcorn, chewing before he continued, "the older one, Claire, is probably only a little younger than me."

David almost added, *and she's gorgeous, like knock the wind right out of you, way out of your league, beautiful.*

Stephen dug into the popcorn bowl too and took a handful. "Do they know what they are going to do yet? Are they sticking around Pismo?" asked Stephen.

"No. Claire mentioned they have seventy-six days to move out of their mom's house and get it up for sale." Amazing how David remembered that very specific detail. He watched as the sun slipped below the water. A stunning smattering of yellow and orange stretched across the sky, and gratitude seeped into David's heart. He continued, "I don't think she lives here, from what I gathered."

Kelly shook her head, starting to knit again. "No, the older one lives in Los Angeles. She's a physical therapist. I only remember because Rebecca always spoke about her with great pride." Kelly tsked, "I still can't believe she's gone, and how she passed. How awful for them. Their dad isn't in the picture either. He abandoned Rebecca before the younger one was born."

Slowly nodding, David pondered on the tragedy of the situation and the unfairness of it. Though his life held challenges, nothing compared to the pain Claire and Alexis experienced. He was grateful to help them in a small way, hoping it relieved a bit of the burden for them.

"Geez, that's definitely a lot to take in," David eventually replied. "But it makes sense why Claire was bringing Alexis to her appointment and not her dad."

A silence lingered, and he focused on the crashing of the

waves against the shore. It was calm and soothing, and David happily remembered the evenings he spent with his parents over the years on this patio, watching the waves. David became acutely aware of how lucky he was to have not one, but two parents in his life.

David stood. "I need to go get something real to eat, besides popcorn. I only wanted to stop by to say hi. Do you want me to take Jasper back in?"

"Yes, thank you, that would be great." Stephen picked up his glasses and e-book and tapped the screen, making it light up again. He put back on his reading glasses. "Have a nice evening."

Kelly bid him goodbye too.

Scooping Jasper back up, David took the yorkie back inside and placed him in his kennel, making his exit for home. David lived only a mile away in a small two-bedroom bungalow, not on the beach like his parents. But he was grateful he'd found something he could afford in Pismo, too. Though it was tiny, it was his.

With his loans from dental school and opening his own practice, David had only recently started to inch his way out of debt. The divorce hadn't helped either. Lauren, his ex-wife, wiped him clean out. He shook the memory of Lauren from his mind. If he lingered too long on her, his heart ached, and shoulders became tense.

Since his divorce three years ago, David had just occasionally dipped his toes back into the dating pool. The experience of having his heart ripped out of his chest wasn't one he was eager to repeat. The only thing pushing him forward was his hope to get remarried and eventually have children of his own. But today, something had happened, a shifting of sorts. When David saw Claire in the waiting room, his heart nearly stopped on sight. His stomach did a weird somersault. Since his divorce, David didn't notice women, but he had noticed Claire. And he didn't want to unpack what it meant.

David picked up some takeout on his way home. Entering his house, he tossed his keys onto the kitchen counter. After removing his pad Thai from the plastic bag, he plopped himself on his couch, relaxing to watch a basketball game while he ate. With a full belly, David cheered his team onto victory, before he dozed off to sleep without ever making it to his bed.

SEVERAL HOURS LATER, DAVID AWOKE TO THE RINGING OF HIS cell phone.

With one eye open, half asleep, he patted the top of the couch, looking for his phone. Once David located it, he clicked accept without checking the number. "Hello?" David rubbed at his sleepy eyes.

Yawning, David double checked the clock on the wall. He hoped he hadn't overslept for work, but then he quickly remembered it was Saturday. His office was closed. Relief washed over him.

"Dr. Clark?" Sarah questioned.

Stretching, David rose, taking his empty to-go container with him. He tossed it into the trash. "Hey, Sarah," leaning against his kitchen counter with his forearms, David asked, "What's up?"

"You sound, out of it," replied Sarah.

"You woke me up," countered David, "and, it's Saturday."

"True..." Sarah's voice faded off. She cleared her throat then continued, "I can see you don't want to be disturbed. I'll tell the patient to go to the dentist. Sorry I bothered you."

"Wait! Sorry..." David rubbed his eyes. More fully wake, he knew he wasn't being as gracious as he should be. Sarah wouldn't call unless it was urgent. She was the one responsible for checking the voicemails for any emergencies that might occur over the weekend. "Who's the patient? And what happened?"

Sarah replied, "Apparently, Alexis… remember she came in with her sister yesterday?" She waited.

His ears perked up a bit. "Yes, of course… go on," said David.

"Alexis fell this morning in dance class, slipped, knocking her teeth on the ballet barre. Her braces slid up and into her top lip and are stuck. Claire said she could try and take her to a dentist if you can't see her today. Do you want me to tell her to do that?"

A second chance to see Claire.

"Let her know I'll meet her and Alexis at the office in a half hour," replied David.

David ended the call and ran to take a shower and change.

Exactly twenty-seven minutes later, David pulled into his office parking lot, parking next to Claire's car. Both were still in it, waiting for him to arrive. Through his window, David waved at the sisters. Claire smiled and waved back, opening her door. His heart rate picked up to a steady staccato beat. *Simmer down.* He partly blamed the adrenaline pulsating through him from the last frantic twenty minutes of showering and changing. The other part—well that was all due to Claire.

Exiting his car, Claire and Alexis lingered by the back of his truck. Claire was in black form-fitting yoga pants and a tank top. Her hair was pulled up into a messy knot. David gulped, forcing himself to concentrate on Alexis, who held a blood-soaked rag to her mouth.

"Oh boy," David motioned for them to follow him to the office's front door. He walked toward the entrance. Over his shoulder, he said, "It looks like the ballet barre won again."

He caught Claire's smirk. The feeling invigorated him.

David made her smile, and he wanted to do everything he could to make it happen again. Fumbling with his keys, he forced himself to pull back his shoulders and focus on getting Alexis the help she needed.

Alexis scoffed, "I didn't know it was a fight," she mumbled through the rag.

"Neither did I." David added without missing a beat. With the correct key found, he opened the door and flipped on the lights to the lobby. "Come on in." He held the door open, allowing them to enter. "I'll survey the damage."

Passing through the door, Claire said, "Thanks for meeting us on such short notice." She wrung her hands together. "I hope we aren't keeping you from your family." She gnawed on her bottom lip.

"Nope," David shook his head. He motioned toward the exam room. "I live alone." He flipped on the lights. "You saved me from a long boring morning of Saturday cartoons." Once at the nearest exam chair, he rested his hands on the head rest. "You can sit here, Alexis."

With the rag still pressed to her mouth, Alexis lowered herself into the chair. "You don't really still watch cartoons… do you?" She raised an eyebrow.

David turned on the overhead exam light, moving it directly over Alexis's mouth. "Of course, I do." Smiling, he gazed over at Claire while he said, "You're never too old to watch cartoons."

"Aren't you like thirty plus?" asked Alexis.

"Alexis," Claire hissed. She closed her eyes for a moment, then patted Alexis on the shoulder. Directing herself to Alexis, Claire continued, "You can't ask things like that." Claire met David's gaze. "Besides, I think Dr. Clark is only teasing you."

Alexis rolled her eyes. "Okay, sorry," muttered Alexis.

"Now, enough about my TV watching habits, and how

I'm way past my prime. Why don't you slowly remove the rag?" David sat down in the swivel chair next to Alexis, grabbing some latex gloves out of the box. He put them on. Claire pulled up one of the other nearby chairs and sat on the other side of Alexis, across from David. "Let me see the damage."

Alexis removed the rag, revealing a swollen and bloody lip. Her top four braces were firmed jammed into her top lip.

"Oh no, ouch." David gasped, drastically. "I hope you'll live."

Alexis's eyes bulged. Her gaze darted to Claire then back to David.

Waving it off, gingerly, David widened her mouth with his fingers. "I'm kidding." David peered closer at her teeth and lip. "This is completely fixable. Your lip will take a while to heal, but there doesn't appear to be any damage to your teeth which should be a huge relief. You're going to get to keep all of them."

Claire sighed, leaning back in her chair. "Thank heavens." Her hand flew to her heart. "I nearly passed out when Alexis showed me her lip."

David caught the train track lines across Claire's forehead slowly easing away. "It always looks worse than it really is." David reverted his attention back to Alexis. "I'm going to need to numb up your lip before I remove these braces stuck in it. Then I'll replace them with new ones. The whole thing should only take an hour or so."

Alexis started to cry. "I'm so glad." She swiped at her eyes. "The last thing I needed was to be toothless too."

"No, no, nothing like that." David patted her shoulder. "You get to keep all your teeth. And when you get these braces off in six months, you'll have a beautiful smile. Let me go grab the numbing medicine and other tools I need, and I'll be right back."

David left and went into the room where the dental instruments were sanitized and stored. He gathered the ones he needed along with the numbing medicine. When he returned to the group exam room, Alexis and Claire were laughing.

David set his instruments down on the side table. He smiled, "I can see you're both in better spirits." He lowered himself onto his swivel stool.

Alexis swiped at the tears running down her face. "Yes, now that I know I'm not going to end up as a toothless teenager, you could say I'm doing better."

Claire continued to chuckle. "Sorry, this is just the first time we've laughed about anything in the past several weeks." With a hand over her belly, her laughing slowly subsided. She swiped at her eyes too. "I'm glad Alexis is going to be okay." She gave Alexis's shoulder a quick squeeze.

"Me too," added David.

Then he shot Alexis up with the anesthetic. Once her lip was numb, he removed the braces and replaced them with new ones. The process was fast and easy. But David found himself having a hard time concentrating with Claire only a few feet away from him. He forced himself not to glance over at her, not once, not even when he felt her eyes on him. But then again, where else was she going to look? So, David tried not to flatter himself too much.

"You can go ahead and sit up." David pressed the button to raise the back of the dental chair. "I'm done."

Once the chair returned to its low position, Alexis swung her legs over the side. "Thank you, Dr. Clark." She wiggled her mouth a little. "My mouth feels so weird." Lightly, Alexis touched her lip.

"Be careful." David stripped his gloves off, gathering up all the used instruments on the metal tray. "Remember, you can't eat anything until the numbness has gone away completely. You don't want to add a bitten cheek to your list of injuries."

Claire stood, gripping her purse. "And how long does it usually take for her mouth to feel normal again?"

"A few hours." David rose too, walking over to a back table, he placed the used instruments in the bin to be cleaned. "Everyone's a little different, but you should be fine by the time lunch rolls around."

Alexis stood. "But, I'm already hungry," she whined.

Claire tilted her head, touching her on the shoulder. "I think you'll manage to survive."

A long pause followed.

David motioned with his hand. "Here, let me walk you out."

Leading them from the exam room to the front door, David held it open for them to exit. Alexis immediately walked to the car without another word. Claire pressed the unlock button on her car keys for Alexis.

Once Alexis was inside with the door closed, Claire glanced over at David. "I know this was extra…" Claire shuffled her feet. "You were so generous to not charge us the remaining balance for her braces. Please let me know how much we owe you for today, and I can settle the bill right now."

David shook his head, shoving his hands into his pockets. "It's on the house."

Claire threw her hands down at her sides. "I can't let you do that. You've already done so much for us already."

"I've done very little." David glanced between the car and Claire. "Besides my mom, Kelly, was friends with Rebecca. Just think of it as a friends and family discount."

"They were? You didn't mention that before." Her face softened, and Claire took a step closer to him. "How did Kelly know Mom?"

With her nearness, David caught a whiff of her sweet intoxicating scent, and his knees nearly buckled. "They were in the same knitting group." David managed to say without his voice shaking.

Slowly nodding, Claire said, "Knitting. Mom did love it. Alexis is wearing a sweater Mom knitted for her." Her voice faded, while her eyes moistened. Claire glanced away, blinking rapidly. "Well, thanks again. I'll let you go." She took one step toward her car then stopped. "Do you have any big plans for the weekend?"

"No, how about you and Alexis?" David asked out of politeness.

"Alexis wants to go see a movie at the outdoor theater on the beach tonight." Claire fiddled with her keys. "It's going to be cold, but she hasn't wanted to do anything lately, so I think I'll take her."

"Is that the one near the pier?" David folded his arms. "I've heard it's fun."

Claire nodded. "I've heard the same thing."

"My parents have mentioned going once or twice. They liked it. I've been meaning to check it out myself," added David.

Claire motioned toward him, "You should join us."

Casually shrugging, David replied, "Thanks. Maybe I will." Though he had zero intention of attending. Claire was only being polite, it was something people said, nothing more.

Walking toward her car, Claire peered over her shoulder and said, "Okay. Thanks again. Bye." She strode the remaining distance to her car. Climbing in, she drove away.

David went back into his clinic to finish cleaning up. The interaction in the parking lot played on repeat in his mind. Should he join Alexis and Claire at the outdoor movie? He shook off the idea. *Nah, ridiculous.*

CHAPTER THREE

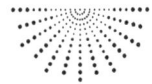

GROANING LOUDLY, CLAIRE SHOOK HER HEAD AS SHE PULLED out of Dr. Clark's office parking lot. "I've made a complete fool of myself." Glancing through the rear-view mirror, the office became further and further away.

What had she been thinking? Was she that desperate for some male companionship she extended invitations to unsuspecting innocent men? *Cringe. Cringe. Cringe.* Claire tapped her forehead with the heel of her free hand.

Alexis sat in the front passenger seat. Progress. Glancing up from her cell phone, she asked, "What did you do now?"

"I practically threw myself at your orthodontist." The words came out in fast spurts. Claire rolled her eyes. "I invited him to join us at the movie tonight." She ran a hand over her head. "What is wrong with me?"

"Did you want me to answer that?" Alexis smirked, clearly enjoying Claire's squirming. "Or are you only thinking out loud?"

The light changed from yellow to red, and Claire slowed to a stop. Tapping her fingers on the steering wheel, Claire tried to dampen the nervous energy pulsating through her.

"Was I acting desperate when you were around? Please say no." She stole a side glance at Alexis.

Alexis shrugged.

Claire continued, "I mean he was the one who said he should check out the outdoor movie." She gnawed on a fingernail. "But I shouldn't have invited him. Who does that? Who invites someone they just met to a movie with their sister?"

Alexis reached out and put a hand on her forearm. "Calm down. I'm sure you didn't act like a fool. So, you think Dr. Clark is hot." She lowered her voice to a calm soothing tone. "It's not a big deal."

Loud, obnoxious sounds oozed out of the radio. Reaching out, Claire flipped it to a different station playing easy listening music. She settled back into her seat waiting for the light to turn.

Pointing, Alexis said, "It's green." Claire drove through the intersection. Alexis continued, "And besides, I'm sure you aren't the first mom to make a move on him." Alexis reached out, changing the radio station again, one playing the newest hits. "Dr. Clark is probably used to all the attention, so I don't think he'll give your invitation a second thought."

Sighing, Claire said, "You're probably right. Now I'm like all those other desperate single moms throwing themselves at him." Her voice faded while her heart sank.

"Stop beating yourself up over the whole thing." Alexis's fingers slid across her cell phone screen. She didn't look up. "There's no way he'll come anyways, so you're in the clear. And you have a whole month until you see him again. Plenty of time for Dr. Clark to forget about the entire interaction."

Suddenly defensive, Claire pushed wisps of hair behind her ear. "Why do you think he won't come?"

As much as she was embarrassed by the conversation with

Dr. Clark, Claire did hold out a tiny bit of hope he'd show. Who didn't want to spend the evening cuddled up next to a smoking hot orthodontist? Geez, her mind was already to cuddling.

"Like you said, he was only being nice." Alexis slid her phone into her pocket then lightly rubbed her hand across her swollen lip. "Is it okay if I invite Juliet? She said her mom can drop her off."

And the conversation about Dr. Clark drifted out the car window with the light ocean breeze. This was the first time Alexis mentioned any of her friends. A few came to the funeral, but Claire, in a full grief-stricken haze, didn't remember any of them. If Alexis wanted to socialize and see her friends again, Claire wanted to encourage it.

"Sure, you can invite Juliet," Claire kept her voice upbeat, "tell her seven o'clock near the pier. We can go straight to the store and pick up some snacks to share."

With not a hint of sarcasm, Alexis said, "Great, thanks Claire."

Claire smiled. For once, she thought, she had managed to make Alexis happy.

∽

LATER THAT EVENING, WITH LAWN CHAIRS IN HAND, CLAIRE peered around the sectioned off area of the beach set up for the outdoor movie. It was showing an old romcom, *You've Got Mail*, one of Claire's favorites. On the other hand, Alexis wasn't thrilled, because she wanted to see the latest blockbuster hit.

"Where should we set up?" Claire surveyed the sand, looking for a spot big enough for them. Hiking up her purse, she attempted to juggle the bag of snacks and lawn chairs. Pointing at a place midway back, Claire nodded her head in the direction. "Does that spot look okay? Do you think Juliet will be able to find us?"

Alexis nodded. "Looks good to me. Here, let me help you." She reached out to take some stuff from her.

Help? Claire's jaw dropped. "Thank you." Claire passed some items to Alexis.

Shrugging, Alexis replied, "You were carrying too much stuff. I should've offered to help back at the car."

Claire couldn't believe the change in Alexis, only this morning she growled at her in the car, but with the prospect of seeing her friend, Juliet, Alexis's entire demeanor changed. Their entire afternoon together, Alexis, was downright pleasant. Next, Alexis offered to help, perhaps the dark cloud looming over them for the last month was starting to lift.

Reshuffling the remaining items, Claire's arms no longer screamed from the weight. "Are you excited to see Juliet? I should've realized you've missed seeing her and your other friends."

"I haven't seen Juliet since the funeral." Alexis walked toward the empty spot. "I think Monday... I should go back to school. It's time. I can't stand sitting around the house any longer missing Mom and constantly being reminded she isn't alive. I miss being around my friends. And I'm sick of doing all the classwork from home." Alexis stopped at the designated place and opened her chair, setting it down on the sand.

For the past month, Alexis had kept up with her schoolwork from home. Claire wondered constantly when it would be a suitable time for Alexis to return to school. Luckily, Alexis came to the decision on her own. Claire placed her stuff down on the sand too, arranging her chair. Promptly, she plopped herself down next to Alexis.

"I think it's a great idea for you to return to school." Claire rubbed her hands back and forth over the top of her jeans to try and stay warm. Thankfully, last minute, she threw on a royal blue sweater Mom had knitted for her. Mom said the color always brightened her face. With the sun nearly gone, the salty ocean air nipped at her skin. "Once your lip is healed, you can start back at the dance studio next week too." She pulled out a blanket from her bag and threw it over her legs.

Some soft music played while they waited for the movie to start. A few minutes later, Juliet arrived, being dropped off by her mom. Soon the two friends chatted to themselves, clearly missing one another. On a whim, Claire dug some cash out of her purse and gave it to the girls to go get some ice cream at the edge of the pier. Claire could see the shop from where she sat. Excitedly, Alexis and Juliet left for the ice cream shop.

With a moment to herself, Claire stared out at the waves crashing on the shore. A wave of happy memories flooded her mind. A mix of memories from her childhood, all were wrapped around the ocean and Pismo Beach. Her finger ran over the tight stitching of the blue yarn of her sweater. Last time she wore it, Claire had gone for a walk with Mom on the beach. Tears tickled the corners of her eyes and soon streamed down her face. Her heart ached and loneliness engulfed her being. She wondered if or when things would get easier. Though she believed Mom was in a better place, Claire still struggled to make sense of everything.

Swiping at her eyes, Claire didn't want Alexis to see her in this state. Luckily, the previews started to play on the big screen, distracting her mind from missing Mom. Halfway into the previews, Alexis and Juliet returned, happily licking their ice cream cones while the rest of the previews played.

Lost in her own depressed state, Claire didn't hear any of the dialogue or music during the previews. Instead, she tuned into the soothing sounds of the ocean. To her surprise, when Claire turned her attention back to the movie screen, the opening credits sprawled across the screen.

Then a hushed whisper called out her name. Claire peered toward the sound, slowly her eyes adjusted from the brighter movie lights to the darkness of the night. Her gaze landed on Dr. Clark, searching the crowd of moviegoers. Reaching her hand up in a wave, Claire locked eyes with him and smiled. Eagerly, he strode the rest of the distance to them. Dr. Clark arrived and crouched down next to her.

Leaning in, Dr. Clark whispered, "I'm glad I found you. I was afraid I wouldn't." He placed his hand on her arm rest, pointing with his other to the empty space next to her. "Is that space taken?"

"Uh, you…" Claire shifted in her seat. Her gaze skidded over his perfectly proportioned frame. Dr. Clark had changed into jeans and a baggy sweatshirt. His dark hair practically glowed under the light of the moon. Her middle pooled with warmth. Oh, dear. With a sudden dry throat, Claire forced herself to swallow and pushed out the words, "You came. I didn't think you would."

Dr. Clark's gaze bore into hers. "I hope that's okay." He blinked, and time stretched into an eternity.

Her heart hammered, sounding in her temples. Instinctively, Claire smoothed out her hair, hating how it flapped wildly with the cool night breeze. "I— I," she stammered.

"Sit down already," someone yelled from behind them.

Shifting around in her seat, Claire craned her neck to see who was yelling. Dr. Clark did the same. She spotted the annoyed patron. The patron glared at her.

Turning back around, Claire leaned in extra close and whispered, "Dr. Clark, you better sit," she patted the top of his hand on her armrest, "or the person behind us might have a conniption."

"Oh, you're right," replied Dr. Clark. He rose quickly, moving to the free space on the other side of her. "I'm sorry."

Dumping his blankets and bag on the sand, Dr. Clark opened his lawn chair and placed it next to her. Once settled in his seat, Dr. Clark leaned forward and waved at Alexis. Alexis's eyes dilated. Slowly, Alexis held up a single hand. Then Alexis and Juliet whispered to one another, though Claire couldn't hear them, she imagined what they were saying. Finally, the whispering stopped, and the girls went back to eating their ice cream cones and watching the movie.

Leaning far over his armrest, Dr. Clark's shoulder touched Claire's. He whispered into her ear, "You can call me David." The words sent goosebumps down her spine.

"David it is." Claire's nostrils flared as his manly scent whirled in the tight space between them. Though it was cold, perspiration smattered her forehead. She gulped. "Thanks for coming." Her words came out shaky.

David blinked, staring at her, he finally replied, "Thanks for inviting me." He broke the touching of their shoulders, straightening his position in his chair.

Casually, with an ease Claire wished she possessed; David propped his ankle across his other knee. The sounds from the movie blared, and David gazed up at the screen. Though Claire wanted to continue to stare at him, she forced herself to look up at the screen too.

For a minute, neither spoke.

Then David shifted back toward her, making their shoulders touch again. She welcomed the warmth trickling down her arm. With a face full of earnestness, David asked, "Is this *You've Got Mail*?"

Claire rested her elbow on the arm rest, moving closer to the warmth of his body. Trying her best to keep her voice low, Claire asked, "Have you seen it?"

"Have I?" Playfully, David elbowed her. "My mom had the

movie on repeat when I was a kid. She's what you may call a bit of a romantic." He smirked, making him a thousand times cuter than seconds prior.

Pulling the old knitted blanket of Mom's on her lap over her shoulders, Claire snuggled down deeper under its cozy layer. "Smart lady," Claire grinned. "I like her already."

David picked up a blanket beside his chair, placing one on his lap. "I have more blankets if you get cold. Do you want another one?"

"I'm okay for now," replied Claire. "I'll let you know if I need it."

With nothing else to say in a hushed tone, Claire reverted her attention back to the movie. With David being so near, Claire couldn't think about anything but him.

Toward the end of the movie, Alexis crouched down next to her chair. "We're bored." She made a pouty face.

Startled, Claire replied, "What?" Peering over at Alexis and Juliet huddled next to her chair, she continued, "Did you already want to go? Juliet's mom won't be here for another hour."

"Can we walk down to the end of the pier?" pleaded Alexis. "We'll come right back. You'll be able to see us the entire time."

Gnawing on her bottom lip, Claire hesitated. She didn't know any of the acceptable parenting rules for a teenager. Was thirteen too young to wander off on your own? Would Juliet's mom be upset if the girls didn't stay right next to her during the movie? Would this wrong parenting move keep Juliet's parents from trusting her in the future? Her mind spun with the worst-case scenarios.

Leaning over her armrest toward Juliet, Claire asked, "Do you think your parents will mind?"

"My mom lets me walk alone to the end of the pier all the time when she's shopping at the little shops on Main Street," whispered Juliet. "As long as she knows where I'm at and when I'll be back."

Claire wondered if Juliet was trustworthy. Wringing her hands together, Claire glanced over at David who appeared to be listening to the entire exchange.

"Do you think it's okay?" asked Claire, shifting her body closer to his, but not touching. "Or do you think her parents will throw a fit when they find out?" She studied him for a reaction.

David shrugged. "I have no clue." He lightly chuckled. "I'm sure it's fine. I remember doing things like that at a way younger age than them."

Mulling it over, Claire shifted back to Alexis and Juliet. "You can walk to the end of the pier and back. I'll watch from here the entire time. Juliet's mom will be here in an hour." She wagged a finger at them. "You better be back in forty-five minutes."

Alexis grinned. "Promise." She jumped up. "Thanks, sis."

Juliet rose too, and the two teenagers took off across the sand toward the pier. Claire watched them until they hit the wooden pier, making sure they were staying in her field of vision.

Leaning close, David whispered into her ear. "I'm sure they'll obey. They both seem like nice girls." Then David pushed a pack of licorice in her direction. "Want some?" He pulled one out for himself and started eating it.

Slipping one out of the package, Claire took a bite. "Thanks," she meekly smiled. "I love licorice."

"Please have as much as you want. Alexis can't have any… or shouldn't be eating it with her braces, so I didn't want to offer it when she was here. I completely forgot about the no candy part of having braces… though I'm constantly reminding my patients about it. You'd think I would've brought something else to share." His voice faded off. David placed the package of licorice on top of his armrest. "Sorry, I'm rambling." Even though it was dark, Claire saw his cheeks redden. He rubbed his hands together. Guess she wasn't the only one who was nervous. "I'll be quiet now." He stared up at the movie screen.

"I like it." Claire finished her first piece of licorice then took another from the pack. Grinning, she continued, "the rambling. It's kind of nice."

Over the past month, most of her interactions with others were heavy, laden with sadness. People offered their condolences, followed up with words of encouragement. It was oddly refreshing to have a normal conversation about something as simple as not eating candy with braces. Claire was grateful for his company. More importantly, she appreciated David treating her like a normal person, and not somebody who was fragile. Plus, his rambling was cute.

Behind them, the lady from before yelled, "Hush down you two. Enough already. I can't hear."

Claire stole a quick glance over her shoulder. The woman glared again, making Claire giggle. Covering her mouth with her hand, she attempted to quiet her laughing.

Her eyes dilated. Touching her shoulder to his, Claire whispered, "She *loves* us."

Nodding, David turned and smiled at the glaring woman. Then he whipped back around. "Sorry," his hand flew to his chest, "my fault. I'll try to not get you into any more trouble."

The rest of the movie played with her in an infatuated haze. Claire remembered to keep Alexis and Juliet in her peripheral view. The movie ended, and the ending credits played across the screen. Immediately, the beach became a buzz of activity as the other patrons quickly packed up their stuff.

Double checking the time, Claire said, "I think I overestimated the length of the movie. I plan on sitting here to wait for Alexis and Juliet to come back. They should be here in fifteen minutes." Claire gazed over at David who remained seated too. "You don't have to wait. I mean you can if you want, but you don't have to."

Geez, she sounded foolish. Claire gripped both of her armrests with her hands as sweat poured down her back. Why was David making her so jittery? It wasn't like she hadn't dated before. But was this even a date when two teenagers were in the middle of it? Probably not.

Steadying her, David placed his hand on top of hers. He locked eyes with her, making her gulp. "I don't mind." His voice was soothing and cathartic, practically whisked away with the ocean breeze. "I'll wait here with you. I'm having a nice time." Then he removed his hand.

Whoosh. Her heart tripled speed, making her warm all over despite the cool night air. Her throat grew tight. "I am too." She fiddled with her curled hair, finally tucking it behind her ears. "I'm having a nice time… with you."

David smiled, putting her further at ease. "Now…" He shifted in his seat, making his shoulder touch hers once again as if imaginary magnets were constantly gravitating their bodies together. "Tell me all about how you ended up in Los Angeles."

"Ahh," Claire smirked. "That isn't a very long story. I went there for college, and then I never came back after I graduated. The end."

"Why didn't you come back after college?" asked David.

"After I graduated, I took a job as a physical therapist at a hospital in Los Angeles. I was dating a guy at the time, and I wanted to see how things would play out. We broke up a year later, but by then I re-signed the lease on my apartment for another year. I liked my job, and I enjoyed working with my colleagues and friends, so I never saw a reason to come back to Pismo. At least not until everything happened…" Claire's voice faded away, and she stared out at the ocean. Sadness wiggled its way back into her being.

David reached out, interlacing his fingers with hers. "I'm glad you're here now." He gave her hand a squeeze. Claire didn't glance over but focused on trying to regain control of her emotions. He continued, "Even if it's for less-than-ideal circumstances."

His words danced between them. A true understatement.

"It's certainly has been less-than-ideal." Her voice cracked. Claire paused for a moment, closing her eyes. "I don't know if things will ever get better." The words a near whisper.

"I'm really sorry," replied David. His thumb ran in circles across the top of her hand. "I don't know what else to say."

Claire sat very still, not wanting to travel down the path which would open the floodgates. They both sat there in their respective silences, staring out at the ocean. The twinkling light of the moon cast a glow against the black darkness of night, Claire wondered how many times she stared at it. Too many times to count, and now the ocean looked different, because her world wasn't carefree like it was in the past.

Breaking the quiet, Claire said, "There's something magical about the ocean don't you think?" She shifted in her seat, leaning in closer to her armrest. "It's the one place I can go and for a minute I breathe lighter, and the tension in my chest lessens."

"I completely agree. I feel blessed to live near the ocean." David rubbed the stubble across his jaw. "I mean whatever is going wrong in my life, I can go take a walk along the beach, and I find a way to sort through my problems. In the early morning, when I have the place practically to myself, it's my favorite time to come here. It helps me clear my mind and find peace and solace. There's something healing about being at the beach."

Then they were abruptly interrupted by the arrival of Alexis and Juliet. Nearly jumping, Claire let go of David's hand.

Smugly smiling, Alexis met Claire's eyes. "We're back and right on time like you asked."

Running a hand over her unruly hair, Claire tucked the strands behind her ears again. "Thanks for sticking to the rules." With a shaky hand, Claire pointed to the chairs, trying to find her equilibrium. "Could you girls help me fold up your chairs? Then we can walk to the parking lot to wait for Juliet's mom. She should be here any minute."

Alexis paused, reading Claire like a book. "Sure," said Alexis. "No problem."

David rose too, folding his chair and gathering his own belongings. After they collected everything, they made their way across the sand to the parking lot. When they arrived, Juliet's mom was idling in her car. Juliet left. They all watched until her car completely exited the parking lot. Once gone, Claire shuffled her feet. David shoved his hands into his pockets.

Shivering, Alexis rubbed her hands together. "Can you unlock the car? I'm cold. I want to run ahead and get warm in the car."

Claire clicked the unlock button, popping the trunk too. Alexis dashed several yards ahead, dumping her stuff in the trunk before she climbed in, leaving David and Claire alone once more.

Dragging her feet, Claire slowed her pace to her car. David matched her speed. She didn't want the night to end, and Claire wondered if David felt similarly. Or if everything was one sided.

Arriving at her car, Claire loaded her things inside the

trunk with David's assistance. Fidgeting with her keys, Claire said, "Thanks for coming tonight. I enjoyed your company."

"I'm glad I came. Thanks for inviting me." David rubbed his jaw then ran a hand through his hair, before settling it into his pocket.

After a beat of silence Claire cleared her dry throat. "I hope to see you again soon."

"Yes," David smiled. "I'd like that."

"Call me," Claire stated. Boy, she was being bold. Bolder than she ever had been before. "Your office has my number."

David pulled his hand out of his pocket, bringing his keys out with it. "Maybe I will," he casually replied. Backpedaling a few steps, he moved toward his truck. "Have a nice night, Claire." He straightened himself, walking the rest of the way.

Without looking again, he left.

With clammy hands, Claire went to her driver's side door. Opening it, she slid into her seat. Stunned, she stared blankly out the windshield.

"Oh..." Alexis giggled breaking her trance. "You've got it bad for Dr. Clark." She shook her head as her fingers zipped across her cell phone. "Juliet thinks you guys look cute together."

Claire's eyes dilated. "What? Were you spying on us?" Her voice rose an octave.

"We didn't have to spy." Alexis kept her gaze glued to her phone. "You were holding hands when we came back from the pier."

Forcing herself to start the car, Claire glanced over her shoulder before backing out of her parking space. "I promise nothing else happened," declared Claire.

"I didn't say anything did." Alexis gave her a sideways glance. "You need to chill out."

"I'm chill." Claire gripped the steering wheel tighter. Her racing heart and sweaty brow begged to claim she was anything but chill. "Besides, David only said he *might* call." She shrugged.

"It's okay." Alexis paused. Her demeanor softened. "You can admit you want him to call. I promise I won't tell."

Claire exhaled, making her shoulders droop. "I want him to call." Peering out her window, she saw her reflection staring back at her. Claire tried to not over analyze her appearance. David either liked what he saw, or he didn't. "But it's totally fine if David doesn't call, because we're leaving Pismo soon..."

"I know we're leaving, but it's okay to still care," replied Alexis without a hint of sarcasm. After a long pause, Alexis added, "and for the record, Dr. Clark would be the lucky one. You are a total catch."

Claire didn't respond though she did appreciate Alexis's kind words. So, Claire had a crush on Dr. Clark… she meant David. None. Of. It. Mattered. Because in seventy-four days, she and Alexis would be gone.

CHAPTER FOUR

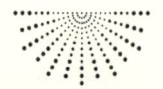

"All done. You can go ahead sit up," said David. He grabbed the patient's chart off the side table and made a few notes. "I think you'll be ready to get your braces off on your next visit."

"Finally," his patient beamed, "I can't wait."

"Let's have you set up your final appointment with Sarah on your way out." David stood, grabbing the patient's chart from the side table. He made some final notes on it.

"Woohoo," the patient declared.

Leading the patient to reception, David gave Sarah the patient's file. Sarah scheduled the last appointment.

After the patient left, Sarah said to David, "Oh, by the way..." She stopped typing and glanced up at him. "Your mom called. She wants you to come for dinner Friday night."

"Dinner?" David couldn't remember the last time his mom, Kelly, called the office for anything. Kelly usually just shot him a text. Many nights he dropped by on his way home from work, not always for dinner, but simply to say hello. "Okay... that's strange." David scratched his head. "I don't know why she didn't call me or text me directly."

Leaning forward, Sarah propped her elbow up on top of her desk, cradling her chin. "She wanted me to check your schedule before I asked you. I think she didn't want you to have an excuse to back out. You're free by the way, and Kelly knows it."

"Wonderful," said David sarcastically. He furrowed his brow. "She's scheming. I can feel it. Do you know what this is all about?"

Sarah held up her hands. "Hey, I only answer the phones. Take this up with Kelly. Unless you want me to call her back for you." Wiggling her mouse, David's schedule popped back on the computer screen. Then Sarah peered back at him. "I could call her back and say something else came up. What do you want me to do?"

David fished his phone out of his pocket. "No," his fingers slid across the screen as he typed a message to Kelly. "I'll get to the bottom of this on my own. Thanks."

Sarah shrugged. Swiveling in her chair, she grabbed some patient files off the shelf.

Though the conversation clearly ended, David couldn't help but elaborate. "Last time Kelly officially made dinner for me, she invited a woman from church to join us. This has a familiar ring to it."

Chuckling, Sarah nodded. "You're probably right. But what can you do? Kelly only wants her son to meet a nice woman. You can't fault her for that." Sarah scooted herself closer to her desk.

David groaned. "I wish she'd stop though."

"You don't even know if she's invited someone," said Sarah. "And besides she's only done it once. It's not like she's trying to set you up left and right."

"Oh, she's invited someone. I know she has." David ran a hand down the length of his face. He knew he needed to get back out there and start dating again, but his most recent dates only left David discouraged. "Anyways…" He stared out the lobby windows, hoping for his next patient to arrive and distract him.

His phone pinged. David dug into his pocket, pulling out his phone. The text revealed Kelly invited some mutual friends for dinner. But before he had time to text back and ask her to elaborate on said friends, the lobby door chimed and in walked his next patient. Greeting the patient, David immediately stopped worrying about his predicament and led them back to the exam room.

The rest of the day sped right on by.

Then the rest of the week. David didn't allow himself to stew over the dinner Kelly set up or call to get more details. Knowing there wasn't any point, David dropped it.

It wasn't until Friday finally rolled around; he dreaded whatever the evening held in store for him. Tugging at his shirt collar, David knocked lightly then entered his parents' house, announcing his arrival as he closed the door behind him.

At the end of the hallway, Kelly popped her head through the sliding glass door. "Come on out here, David." Her voice carried down the long corridor. Waving him over, Kelly continued, "we'll eat out here tonight. It's too nice a night to be stuck inside."

When David didn't immediately move, Kelly entered the house walking toward him.

Striding down the hallway, David met her halfway. "Who did you invite?" asked David, keeping his voice low enough not to carry out the open sliding door. Darting his glance between Kelly and the outside voices, he continued, "and why wouldn't you tell me who you invited? What's with all the secrecy?" He suddenly wanted at least a slight heads up before he faced whoever was beyond the door.

Fluffing her hair, Kelly pushed up her chin. "It's like I said… a mutual friend… actually friends."

David raised an eyebrow, tilting his head to the side, he studied Kelly. "What *friends?*"

Kelly tugged on his arm, bringing him closer. Lowering her voice, she replied, "I invited Claire and Alexis. After you told me you were Alexis's orthodontist, I felt the need to do something nice for Rebecca's girls. So, I drove on over to the house, I went there many times for the knitting circle I was in with Rebecca, and I extended them an invitation."

David inhaled. His eyes darted toward the patio. Laughter vibrated down the hallway. Kelly had no clue he had joined Claire and Alexis at the beach for a movie. Now he regretted not calling or at least texting. Though David enjoyed Claire's company and found her attractive, he didn't see the point in meeting up again, not with her moving.

Shaking his head, David pinched the bridge of his nose. "Why didn't you just tell me that?" He gritted his teeth.

His heart jackhammered. Sweat slathered his brow. Claire was out there… geez this was a mess. David cringed at how little he thought through the consequences of joining Claire and Alexis at the movie. Naïvely, after the movie, he thought he could avoid Claire until they left Pismo. Now the error in his thinking was blaring obviously.

"I didn't want you to fight me on it," countered Kelly. Nudging him with her elbow, Kelly continued, "besides you should be glad. It's not like I'm trying to set you up. I only needed someone closer in age to them, so the conversation was a little livelier."

"Fine," David's jaw locked. "Do Claire and Alexis know I'm coming? Did you tell them I'm Alexis's orthodontist?" His middle twisted on itself.

Kelly slapped him on the arm. "Of course, I told them."

She gave him a sideways glance. "Why do you look pale suddenly? What am I missing here?"

David gulped. *This was going to be awkward.* Sweat smattered his brow. He swiped it away, forcing himself to smile. Kelly narrowed her eyes, reexamining him.

Motioning his head toward the patio, David mustered up some courage. "You aren't missing anything." He cleared his throat, squaring his shoulders. "I'll follow you out to the patio."

Pivoting, Kelly wandered back to the patio. David followed behind her. Before he passed through the screen door, he took a deep breath to settle the rapid pace of his heartbeat. Once through the sliding door to the patio, David closed it behind him before turning to face everyone. When he finally glanced over, Stephen, Claire, and Alexis stopped talking and stared back at him. David gulped. Alexis crossed her arms and glared. Claire's back stiffened, but she met his gaze and held it.

Dang, Claire looked good. Her hair was down, loose, and flowy. And her jeans and T-shirt managed to hug her in all the right places. Oh, buddy. David tried to remember why he blew it and didn't call her. Then he reminded himself they were moving from Pismo.

"Hello to you both," David forced his lips into a crooked smile. "I hope you're having a nice evening."

Lowering himself into the only available seat next to Claire, he awkwardly sat down.

"David," Claire folded her arms. "It's nice to see you again. Or should I call you Dr. Clark?" Her gaze seared his skin, making him all sorts of nervous.

Gulping, her words sent a shiver down his spine. "David is fine," he managed to reply. David scooted his chair closer to the table, trying his best to act casually. Claire being this near him made him acutely aware of his appearance. "I hope you are doing well since the last time I saw you."

"We're great." Alexis piped up. Her gaze darted to Claire, looking for confirmation. "Right?"

"You bet," Claire turned her face away from David, staring out at the view of the ocean. "Never better."

The sound of the waves competed against the commotion in his chest. David was at a loss for what else to say. He imagined the evening was going to be a long one. He gazed out at the view too, trying to think of something else to talk about.

If Kelly noticed the tension between them, she didn't acknowledge it. Pushing her chair back, it scraped against the floor. "Stephen, why don't you help me bring out the dinner."

David moved to get up too. "Do you need more help?" He certainly wanted an opportunity to escape for a moment and dampen the anxiety bubbling up inside of him.

Kelly waved him off. "No, we can manage. You stay and talk to the girls."

Perfect.

Begrudgingly, David settled back into his chair. Stephen and Kelly left to get the food, leaving David to face the mess he made.

More silence.

His skin itched. David tugged at his shirt collar.

Claire spoke up first. "I didn't know Kelly and Stephen were your parents, not until I arrived." Claire kept her gaze on the ocean. The ocean breeze filtered in between them. She looked beautiful, and suddenly her departure day whisked away with the wind. He wondered why he worried about something so trivial. "Kelly was nice enough to invite us over. She made it difficult to refuse." Glancing down, she fiddled with the ends of her shirt. "It wasn't until we arrived, she mentioned who you were and that you would be joining us."

Alexis scoffed. "Yeah, we wouldn't have come." Her eyes glued to her phone. Alexis didn't bother looking up. "Trust me."

David ran his hands back and forth over the chair's armrests. "I don't imagine you would. I didn't know either. I mean Kelly wouldn't tell me who she invited."

"Your parents seem like very nice people." Claire shifted, turning to meet his eyes. It nearly undid him right then and there. "Let's not mention us going to the movie together. I think it's for the best." She waved a hand, reverting her glance back to the ocean. "In fact, let's forget it ever happened."

Boom. Whoosh.

Slouching, David replied, "If that's how you want it…"

Though David had no idea what he wanted, even though he had fallen asleep every night that week thinking about his conversation with Claire on the beach. They were interrupted by David and Kelly, pushing open the sliding door with their hands full of food. David jumped up to assist them with placing the food on the table. Kelly had prepared grilled chicken, corn on the cob, fruit salad, and baked potatoes. With everything on the table, they resettled into their seats. Stephen offered a quick prayer over the food.

Slowly, they passed the food around in a circle. Each took some of each dish. It seemed to David that Claire was extra diligent in making sure their hands didn't touch when handing him the next plate of food.

While spooning some fruit salad onto her plate, Kelly said to Claire, "David told me you were moving." Stephen took the fruit bowl from her and took some for himself. Kelly reached for the corn on the cob and took one. "Do you have a moving date?"

Nodding, Claire replied, "Yes. My job is on hold for me in Los Angeles. We can't afford to stay here." Claire took the baked potatoes from Alexis, placing one on her plate before holding them out to David. Once he took one and passed them to Stephen, Claire continued, "We have about sixty-six days to be out of my mom's house before we put it up for sale."

Alexis crossed her arms. "I can't believe you're making me move," she muttered.

Claire's back stiffened. Swiping at the loose hairs around her temples, she tucked them behind her ears. "I know it isn't ideal." Claire reached out, giving Alexis's shoulder a squeeze. Claire sighed, making her chest heave and shoulders droop. "But we don't have a choice."

Lifting her shoulder, Alexis shook off Claire's hand. Removing her hand, Claire picked up her fork and scooted around some food around on her plate. Alexis pierced a piece of chicken, shoving it into her mouth. The silence between the two sisters permeated the very air they breathed.

Taking a sip of his drink, David broke the tension and said, "I've heard great things about Los Angeles." David speared a piece of chicken. "They don't call it the city of stars for nothing. You do ballet, Alexis, just think of the huge dance studios they have there. There'll be way better opportunities for you in Los Angeles to dance than here in tiny Pismo. It might turn out better than you ever imagined."

Alexis's eyes lit up. "How did you know I did ballet?"

Casually, David grabbed his corn on the cob. "I fixed your lip didn't I? Plus, you've told me, multiple times about your dance at your orthodontist appointments." He took a bite.

Pausing, Alexis blinked. "Yeah," her tone softened. Her icy exterior from earlier melted away. "But, Dr. Clark, you have like hundreds of patients. I can't believe you remember I danced."

David shrugged. "I remembered." He wiped his face with his napkin. "I could tell by how you spoke about it that it was a passion of yours."

Alexis shifted forward. "Do you think I could be discovered there? I've always wanted to become a professional ballerina, but I never dreamed it could be possible." Her eyes widened with anticipation.

"They discover people in Los Angeles all the time. It's the perfect place to go." David had no clue if that was true or not, but it seemed like the right thing to say. His gaze skidded to Claire. She tilted her head, shifting closer to him and mouthed *thank you.* David smiled, turning his attention back to Alexis. "So, what's your favorite part of ballet?"

Alexis lit up like fireworks. Her entire being beamed as she told him about her love of ballet. Kelly and Stephen jumped in and asked a few more questions. Claire's demeanor softened, and she no longer avoided his glance.

As the meal finished up, Kelly asked, "What are you going to do with your mom's stuff? Do you need help packing?"

Claire sighed, clasping, and unclasping her hands on top of the table. "I'm going to sell the big things we can't take with us." She flipped her hair over one of her shoulders. "Some I'll move into storage. And the remaining items I think we can fit into my apartment in Los Angeles, we'll take with us."

"I'm sure you'll need lots of help packing and organizing everything," added Stephen.

"I'll manage." Claire shrugged, taking a sip of her water. "Alexis is at school during the day, and I'm on leave from my job. Every day I get a little bit more done."

"I don't doubt you are more than capable." Kelly placed her silverware on top of her empty plate. "But you'll need some help with moving the big things." She made a head nod toward David. "David can help you with whatever heavy lifting you might need. He's still relatively young." She nudged him with her elbow.

Uncrossing his ankles, David raised an eyebrow. "Thanks, Mom? I think..." Pausing, he shifted in his seat. David turned toward Claire. "But yes Claire, I'd be happy to help you out with whatever you need."

Waving her hand, Claire avoided his gaze, staring out at the ocean. "I'll be fine. Besides I'm sure David has better things to do with his time than helping me."

After remaining mostly silent for the duration of their exchange, Alexis piped up and asked, "What about the yard sale next Saturday?"

Without even giving David time to reply, Kelly piped up, "David can help you with your yard sale. He doesn't have a life and doesn't work Saturdays."

David threw a pointed look at Kelly. Kelly narrowed her eyes at him and dared him to challenge her. Leaning forward, David steepled together his fingers, resting his elbows on the table. "I'd be happy to help. I can come next Saturday to assist you with your yard sale." He moved closer to her. "You'll need help moving the big stuff outside to your driveway, right?"

Claire ran a finger in a circular motion around the top of her glass. "I suppose I do need help." Each word was slow and calculated.

"I have ballet Saturday morning, so I can't help," added Alexis. "So, please don't turn down David's willingness if you are counting on me to pitch in."

Gnawing on her bottom lip, Claire paused. "Saturday, are you positive you don't mind?"

"Nope." David clapped his hands together. "It's all settled then. What time do you want me there?"

CHAPTER FIVE

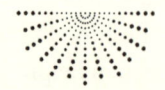

"Do you have everything you need for your ballet class?" Claire shoved some snacks into a paper bag for Alexis to take with her.

Alexis's Saturday dance classes were twice as long, and even more expensive than the ones she took during the week. Claire didn't know how long her finances would last to allow Alexis to attend the dance studio. The yard sale might help a tad with their cash flow. Hopefully in Los Angeles, Claire could find some more affordable options. Her shoulders tightened, and Claire craned her neck back and forth to loosen it.

Grabbing the paper bag from Claire, Alexis pushed it into her duffle bag. "Did you packet those almonds I like?" asked Alexis. Then Alexis zipped her bag closed, placing it on her shoulder.

"I packed double, along with extras of the other things you enjoy. You'll be there until lunch." Claire leaned back against the kitchen counter. "Juliet's mom offered to bring you home too, because she knows I'll be busy finishing up with the yard sale. I told her I could drive carpool next week."

Snagging a banana from the fruit bowl on the kitchen counter, Alexis peeled back the top and took a bite. "Do you think you'll sell a lot of stuff?"

Shrugging, Claire replied, "No idea." She shifted her weight, crossing her ankles. "But I hope so. We need the money to hire a U-Haul to bring the remaining things to Los Angeles."

Alexis shoved two more bites of banana into her mouth before tossing the empty banana peel into the trash. "I'm still pretending we aren't moving."

Luckily, the doorbell chimed, interrupting them. Claire straightened herself, holding up a finger. "Juliet's mom is here." Claire hurried Alexis to the door. "Let's not keep her waiting."

Alexis left.

With Alexis off to ballet, Claire went straight to work, taking the last of the random items to be sold to the garage. During the week, she had gone room by room packing up and determining what to sell, keep, or donate. The bigger furniture she still needed David's help to move. Wandering into the garage with the last box of stuff, Claire set it down and pressed the garage door opener.

Slowly, the garage door retracted, rolling up, revealing a smiling David standing in the driveway with a box of donuts in one hand and a travel mug in the other.

David ducked under the still moving door. "Good morning," said David cheerfully. "How are you doing this fine morning?" He grinned brightly enough to make his eyes twinkle in the corners.

Claire couldn't help herself as her eyes slid down the length of his body. Oh dear... David looked extra hot this morning in his joggers, sweatshirt, and baseball cap. Forcing herself to move and not stare, Claire weaved her way through the messy garage, stopping a few feet from him.

With a hand on her hip, Claire simply said, "So... you're one of those annoying morning people. Aren't you?" Her voice came out all weird and overly high with her pathetic attempt to flirt.

Calm down. Calm down. Calm. Down.

Holding her gaze, David took a sip from his travel mug, before he replied, "Only when I get to see you."

A tingle slid down her spine. Her cheeks burned, no doubt making a streak of red down her entire neck. Claire chose to ignore his flirtatious comment, reminding herself he was the one who didn't call. This was David. A shameless flirt, someone who had a natural repertoire with women and was naturally charming. None of it meant he liked her back.

"Thanks for coming to help." Claire avoided his gaze, choosing instead to glance past him toward the street. "I appreciate it." Then she peered around the garage packed with stuff. "But, I think Kelly volunteered you for more than you bargained for."

David took another sip from his travel mug. He shrugged. "Nothing I can't handle." Then he flipped open the lid of the donuts with the bottom of his travel mug, revealing a dozen assorted donuts. The tantalizing aroma of sugar tickled her nostrils, making her suddenly aware of her lack of any sort of breakfast. "Donut?"

Taking two steps closer, Claire peeked inside. "I don't know how I'll choose. You've brought all my favorites. But I'm a sucker for a chocolate bar." She reached in and grabbed it. "Thanks." Smiling, she held it up then took a bite.

David dug out a napkin packed into the side of the box and held it out to her. "I've always had a weakness for chocolate sprinkles. There's no other way you can basically eat cake for breakfast, and nobody will question you."

Claire laughed, easing the tension in her gut. "You're totally right. I never thought about it that way."

Smirking, David took another sip from his travel mug. Then David set his mug and box of donuts down on a waist high pile of boxes, digging into the box of donuts himself. Taking a chocolate sprinkled donut, David ate it in three bites.

Wiping his fingers off on a napkin, David said, "Okay... now that we've been properly set up for a sugar crash, you need to put me to work before that happens." He tipped up his baseball cap, making the edge of his hair hang out. "What do you need me to do first?"

Finishing up the last bites of her donut, Claire wiped her face with a napkin, then crumpled it up, shoving it into her pocket to throw away later. "I think we should first move the stuff from the garage out to the driveway. It will make space for the furniture I need to move from the house to outside."

Readjusting his baseball cap, David clapped his hands together and rubbed them. "Let's do this. I'm completely counting this as my workout for the day."

"Me too... though I rarely work out," replied Claire.

David's gaze slid over her, making her body buzz. "It certainly doesn't show... you had me fooled."

Claire hesitated. She wasn't as skilled at flirting, so Claire simply twisted toward the beginning of the piles of stuff that needed to be moved. Quickly, they worked together to bring things out to the driveway, unpacking them and placing them on tables for people to better view what was for sale. Once the garage was cleared out, Claire led David into the house. Claire pointed out the furniture items needing to be moved. They worked in tandem with one another.

In the middle of moving the last sofa, Claire held one end of it with both hands. "I didn't realize how much stuff I needed to sell," said Claire.

David grunted.

Claire continued, "I think this can be the last piece of furniture. I need to keep at least one couch for us to use for the remainder of our time here."

David didn't respond but remained focused, maneuvering the sofa around odd angles and corners.

Claire rambled on, "I'll have to do another garage sale before we move out."

Sweat glistened on David's brow. "That's probably a good idea," he finally replied. He shifted the weight of the sofa. "We need to angle this end to get it through the door to the garage."

Her arms screamed against the weight of the couch. "Okay, I'm ready." Claire lifted her end higher while David crouched down at the other end, navigating it seamlessly through the door.

Once through the doorway, they walked the remaining steps to the driveway, plopping the sofa down on the last empty piece of concrete. Wiping his hands on his jogger pants, David then held his hand up in a high five. "Great job." Claire high fived him back. "I'm impressed with how strong you are."

Flushed, Claire smiled. "Thanks."

People started to arrive, rifling through the piles of stuff at the far end of the driveway. Meandering further out, Claire greeted some of the neighbors who stopped by to look. "Everything must go." Claire waved her hands over a table of trinkets. "I'm ready to give you some deals."

David came up beside her. His nearness made the hairs on her arms stand straight up. Claire sidestepped away from him, widening the gap between them to help her mind clear. Soon she became busy helping those shopping. David jumped in too, assisting some neighbors who asked about a pair of side tables. Double checking with Claire,

David sold the tables then moved onto another pair shopping.

The first few hours flew by. David proved to be extra helpful, moving sold items into the back of people's pickup trucks. When there was a lull in shoppers, David spent the time rearranging items, moving things to better positions to be seen from the curb. Claire couldn't help but stare in awe at his ease around others. Everyone he helped ended up laughing and talking to him like they were old friends and not perfect strangers. He was the exact opposite of Claire, who was stressed and anxious the entire time.

As the garage sale wound down, they relaxed in the two foldable beach chairs Claire didn't want to sell. Exhausted, Claire slumped further into her chair, crossing her ankles. David sat, cupping the back of his head with his hands. Claire stared out at the mostly empty driveway. Luckily, most of the bulky items sold, and only random knickknacks remained.

Smiling, David leaned back further, crossing his ankles too. He shifted, tilting his head toward her, he said, "I had no idea how many people go to garage sales in this town." Removing his hands from the back of his head, David tapped the tops of the chair's armrests with both hands. "I think I've seen at least ten of my patients' parents."

Shrugging, Claire replied, "Everyone likes a deal."

Claire didn't want to think about the items from her childhood home scattered across Pismo. The thought made her sorrowful. It was hard enough to watch her mom's precious things go. She was grateful Alexis was at ballet, so she didn't have to witness people haggling over her mom's clothing and trinkets. The air in her lungs became tight and shallow. Grief pushed its way back into her being. Claire looked away, blinking rapidly. Her eyes tickled with the forming of tears.

David sat straight up, shifting closer to her, without saying anything he placed a hand on top of hers. The minutes ticked right on by. No new customers came to interrupt them. Instead, they sat in the quiet stillness. Claire focused on regaining control of her emotions.

Claire finally broke the silence. "I wish I didn't have to sell most of my mom's things but, I've no choice." Her voice cracked. "We need the money, and it won't all fit in my apartment in Los Angeles."

Giving her hand a gentle squeeze, David said, "I can't imagine how hard this has been for you. I'm sure the burden you've been carrying can't be easy. I wish I knew what else to say." David squeezed her hand once more. "But you'll get through it." He dropped his hand, folding his arms against his body.

Claire wanted to scream—impossible. Her life felt too shattered to ever get easier.

David brought his foot up, propping it on his other knee. "Please let me know what else I can do to help you. I'll wait while you think of something..."

Claire paused, closing her eyes for a moment. After a few deep breaths, she replied, "You've helped more than you know."

During their exchange, Claire hadn't noticed a neighbor approaching. A voice asked for the price on a birdhouse, startling them both. Claire flinched then sprang into action, jumping up and moving to the end of the driveway where her neighbor stood. She told them the amount and collected the payment. Soon her neighbor was on their way, and David and she were alone once more.

Shoving the money into her pocket, Claire put her hands on her hips. "I think we should call it a day." Claire faced David. "What do you think?" She raised an eyebrow.

"Whatever you say, boss." David stood up all businesslike.

The moment of intimacy from prior dissipated with the cool ocean breeze. "What should we do with your remaining stuff?"

Claire took in the smattering of things left out. It wasn't much, but if she thought about it too long, she'd start to cry. Mom's quilting supplies, her water skis, along with lots of her clothing. "Let's put it back into the boxes, and I'll take it to Goodwill. Sometime…" Her voice faded, hoping she'd find the courage to follow through with the last step.

"I brought my truck in case you needed help moving anything." David fiddled with the bill of his baseball cap, tipping it up a bit. "How about we load the things directly into there? It'll save you time if we take the things over today. One less thing to worry about." He waited for her to answer.

Gnawing on her bottom lip, Claire checked her watch. "It might be tight." She ran a hand over her hair. "Alexis is getting dropped off in an hour from ballet. Do you think we can make it?"

"If we load everything up, and you don't have time to go with me…" David rubbed the stubble on his jaw. "I can take the things to Goodwill for you. I don't mind."

Claire wanted to argue, but David had a point. And she needed his help. His kindness made her like him even more than before. She wished to find some sort of fatal character flaw in David, anything that would make it easier for her to not be attracted to him. It wasn't his fault he didn't have any romantic interest in her.

"Thanks…" Claire managed. Her voice came out shaky. "You'd save me a lot of time and trips."

With a nod, David replied, "Okay then, let's get to work." He walked toward his truck and opened the back.

David moved first, walking back toward the driveway, grabbing her mom's old skis. Claire grabbed a box and took it to the truck, placing it on the bed. David and Claire worked in silence, packing up the remaining items. After a few trips to his truck, the driveway and the garage were cleared.

Claire wiped her sweaty and dusty hands on her jeans. "I certainly owe you for your help today. A million thanks."

"It was my pleasure." Warmly, David smiled, making her middle a gooey mess. "And…" His eyes twinkled with mischievousness. "It's like Kelly said, I really don't have anything else going on."

Claire chuckled, forcing the nerves in her stomach to settle. "I think you're only being modest." She popped a hip, putting a hand on it. Without thinking, she waved a hand over the length of his body. "A single good-looking guy like you, I don't believe that nonsense for a second."

Smirking, David took a step closer, their bodies two inches from grazing each other. Electricity buzzed between them. "You think I'm good-looking?" He locked eyes with her.

Her cheeks burned. Claire shuffled her feet, shoving her hands into her pockets. She half stumbled a step backward. "Come on." Claire regained her balance. "It's not anything you haven't heard before."

David blinked. He spoke slowly, emphasizing each word. "You've got it completely wrong. If anyone is good looking here, it's you."

Heat wiggled its way down her spine. "I— I—" Claire stammered. "Thanks?"

Her phone in her pocket rang, interrupting their flirtatious exchange. Claire shifted away from David. With a shaky hand, she pulled her phone out of her pocket and saw Alexis's name light up across her screen.

Answering, Claire ran a hand over the top of her messy hair. "Hi, Alexis. Are you on your way home?" She gnawed on the inside of her cheek. Her daze darted to David then away again.

"Can I go to the outlet mall with Juliet?" asked Alexis. "Her mom says it's okay if I go with them. Please?" she pleaded.

David leaned against his truck, crossing his arms. He waited.

"Sure. What time do you think you'll be back?" asked Claire.

In the background, Claire heard Alexis asking Juliet's mom for the details. A few moments later, Alexis said, "She said she'll take us to lunch then shopping. So, I should be back between three and four."

Claire agreed to the plans and ended the call. Shoving her phone into her back pocket, she pushed up the sleeves of her shirt. "Alexis is going to lunch and shopping with Juliet. She'll be gone for a few more hours. I guess I have time to take this stuff to Goodwill. If that still works for you?"

David straightened himself. "Yep, works for me." He moved to the passenger side door and held it open. "Let's go."

Claire closed the distance between them, climbing into the truck. David waited until she was safely inside.

"Thanks." Claire croaked. Her throat was suddenly dry and restricted. Heat smeared across her face and chest. "I appreciate it."

"My pleasure." Then David closed the door and went around the driver's side, climbing in next to her.

Buckling her seat belt, Claire sensed the intimacy of the truck bench. Inside it was tight, and Claire was only a few inches from David. Claire reminded herself he wasn't interested in her. David had placed her firmly into the friend's camp when he didn't contact her after the movie on the beach. And today, David was a nice guy, helping.

David started his truck, making the soothing melody of

Jason Mraz fill the quiet of the truck cab. Casually, David placed his arm along the back of the seat bench to back out. His fingertips brushed the top of her shoulder, making Claire suck in the air. Surely, David felt the fireworks too, right? She stole a glance at him. Wrong. David remained stoically undeterred. His movements were methodical, once in the proper direction, he removed his arm, continuing down the street at a slow steady speed.

The residential neighborhood of her childhood passed by in a haze. Claire transported her thoughts away from David and back to the many memories wrapped up tightly inside of her. Grief engulfed her being. The familiar streets were riddled with memories at every turn. Each street and place they passed, an old experience wiggled its way to the surface like walking to Main Street for saltwater taffy, riding their bikes to the pier, pushing Alexis in the stroller down the sidewalk, and on and on her head twirled with the nostalgia of the past. Claire missed Mom so much her chest ached.

With no ability to push away the sadness, tears streamed down her cheeks. Claire swiped them away with the ends of her sleeves. Coming to a halt at the red light, David glanced between the windshield and her. Claire stared down at her hands in her lap, wishing for the brokenness inside of her to be pieced back together. They said time healed all wounds, but maybe hers were too deep to ever repair. Maybe she'd always be broken.

Clearing his throat, David's voice startled her. "If you need them, there's a pack of tissues in my glovebox."

Swiping a few more tears away, Claire reached out and dug around in the glovebox until she located the small travel size pack of tissues. She peeled back the plastic top and took one out. "Thanks." Claire dabbed at the corners of her eyes. "I didn't think I would get so emotional… it was way harder than I thought parting with my mom's things." She exhaled, turning her face away from him, staring out the passenger side window.

The light turned green. David drove through the intersection. "I can't imagine," He paused, making a right-hand turn. "For what it's worth, I think you're incredibly resilient. I'm in awe of how much you've handled on your own, but you've managed to do it while gracefully taking on the care of Alexis. It's truly commendable."

Claire blew her nose. The tightness in her chest settled, easing the pinch between her shoulder blades. "It doesn't feel that way." Turning in her seat, Claire twisted halfway to glance over at him. "Most of the time I feel like I'm one step away from drowning. Like one last thing will push me all the way under."

Hand over hand, David maneuvered his truck into the parking lot of Goodwill. He pulled into a spot and turned off the ignition, making the radio turn off with it. Suddenly, it became very still. Placing one arm around the back of the bench seat, David exhaled. He fiddled with his keys before shoving them into his pocket.

"I'm sure it does feel like you're drowning. Tragedies can do that to a person." Running a hand down his face, David paused, keeping his glance straight out the windshield. "I know I haven't lost a parent, but I did lose someone I loved very much..." His voice trailed off.

He seemed to be a thousand miles away.

"Tell me about them," said Claire. "I mean, if you don't mind sharing."

A long exhale made his chest heave. David turned back toward her, running a single finger across the fabric seat in the scant inches between their two bodies. "When I was in high school, after homecoming my senior year, me and my friend, Blake, were coming back from the dance." His gaze flickered to hers, and the pain in his eyes nearly undid her.

David stopped running his finger on the seat and rubbed his jaw. "Blake was driving. It was dark, and Blake took a turn too fast. We skidded right off the road and down the embankment."

A long pause followed. Claire wasn't sure if he was going to continue. David broke their gaze and stared blankly out the windshield. His voice cracked, "Blake died, and I lived. I lived, but for a long time it didn't feel like living. It felt like a life sentence."

"I'm so sorry," whispered Claire.

David's confident exterior melted away, and Claire desired deeply to pull him into an embrace.

Gripping his chest, David said, "That's what I've got to deal with. I lived. He died. I'm here. He's not. For years, I felt so guilty. Why was I the one who was saved? Blake was a way better guy than me. He was All-American in football, straight A's, always the first to offer help to those who needed it. I wasn't anybody special." David pulled his gaze from the window. "But..." he spoke slowly. "Sometimes we never get to find out the why. We only get to learn how to move past it, how to live with the pain, how to create a life without them in it. So yes, you may feel like you're drowning, but someday you'll come up for air. Nobody knows how long it'll take. It's different for everyone when it comes to grief. For me it took a long time, but one day I woke up and realized I was finally on the other side of it. I realized I was going to be okay. I realized for whatever reason, God let me live and I needed to appreciate the gift of just... living. And though it doesn't seem like it right now, someday you'll be okay too. I promise."

Exhaling, Claire gnawed on her bottom lip. "Thanks for telling me about... Blake. I can't imagine how difficult that was for you." She reached for his hand, but stopped herself in time and placed her palm flat against the fabric of the bench.

"It was awful." David shifted, resting his arm along the back of the bench, his hand grazed the top of her shoulder. "I haven't talked about it in years, but my whole point in telling you was, I didn't think I'd ever move on. I thought I would be treading water forever, but eventually I was able to breathe again. You will too. Little by little, things will get better, more bearable." His hand shifted more, cupping her shoulder.

Claire leaned into the warmth of his skin, allowing David to comfort her in this small way. "I don't know if I can forgive God for taking Mom from Alexis and me." Claire pinched the bridge of her nose. "The injustice of it is eating me alive."

"You've certainly had a heavy load to carry. I know when I lost Blake, one day I finally decided to give my anger, sadness, and despair back to God. I let him carry it, because it was too difficult for me to do on my own," said David.

"I know. I've been trying." Claire shifted a tad closer to him. "This is the hardest thing I've ever done."

Reaching out, David tucked the hair framing her face behind her ear. "I'm sure it is, more than most will ever have to do, but at least with Him, you know it's possible."

Claire agreed. An awkward silence followed. The lines between friendship and more were all muddled. She didn't trust herself.

Unbuckling her seat belt, Claire moved away from the intoxicating feeling of his touch. "Should we unload everything?" She raised an eyebrow. "I've already eaten up most of your Saturday. I don't want to keep you out any longer."

"Yes, of course." David unbuckled his seatbelt and climbed out.

CHAPTER SIX

Turning onto Claire's street, a fire raged in David's gut. After spending the entire day with Claire, David couldn't fight the feelings he was developing for her. The tight, intimate space of the truck bench didn't help things either. His mind raced with his wildest fantasies, with Claire smack dab in the middle of them.

Pulling to a stop in front of her house, David turned off the truck. With shaky hands, he swiped at the perspiration smeared across his brow. Tipping up his baseball cap a bit, David tried to appear cool and collected.

Slowly, Claire unbuckled her seatbelt. "Thanks again for your help today." Lingering, she rubbed her hands back and forth over the top of her thighs. "I appreciate it."

"Anytime," replied David. His temples pulsed, making it difficult for him to think straight. Somehow, he managed to add, "Let me know if you need any more help clearing stuff out or moving things. I'm happy to help."

"I'm sure I'll need more help at some point." Claire gripped the doorknob, pushing open the passenger side door. She paused, looking over her shoulder at him. "Do you want to come in for a while? I could make you something for lunch. You certainly earned a free meal."

Glancing at his watch, David contemplated what to do. He wanted to spend more time with Claire, heck, he wouldn't mind kissing her either. Then the truth stopped him cold; Claire was leaving in two months. It wasn't worth risking his heart by getting attached. Look at how long it had taken him to get over his ex-wife, three long hard years. Quickly, his heart packed itself back up.

"Thanks for the offer." David cleared his throat. "But I have some other stuff I need to get done today that I've neglected."

Her face fell, making his stomach twist on itself. Claire climbed the rest of the way out of the truck. Shifting back, she said, "Of course, I'll let you get to it. I'll see you around, David."

David blinked. "Yes," he gulped. "I hope to run into you soon."

Claire said goodbye and closed the door, wandering up the walkway to her front door. David watched her slip into the house before he started the car and drove away. His shoulders slumped.

Instantly, David regretted not taking Claire up on her offer of lunch. How did the repercussions of his divorce still have this grip on him? It wasn't right. For a few blocks, David wrangled with his range of feelings. *It's better this way. She's leaving. You'll only end up alone. There's no point in lunch, you'll only want to see her again.*

At the next light, against his own arguments, David made a U-turn and drove the entire way back to Claire's house. After parking, David jogged up to her front door. Heart racing, breathless, David rang the doorbell. He pressed his flat palmed hand against the wall next to the door, regaining his breath while he waited for Claire to answer.

Soon, the door swung open revealing Claire. Her face lit up, unraveling the ball of nerves in his gut. Tilting her head to the side, her glance slid down him. Eagerly, Claire asked, "Did you forget something?"

"No." David shook his head, standing straight, he squared his shoulders. "Nothing like that," he stammered. *Don't chicken out now.* "Can I take you to lunch?"

Claire fiddled with the ends of her sleeves. "I can't let you do that. You helped me, remember. Besides, I thought you were busy." She gnawed on the inside of her cheek.

David removed his baseball cap, running a hand through his messy hair. "If I'm being honest..." his voice faded. He rubbed at the stubble on his jawline. "I like being around you. I don't know what I was thinking earlier by refusing your offer, but I'm free and I want to buy *you* lunch."

Shuffling her feet, Claire glanced back into her house. "Okay," she held up a finger, "give me a second to grab my purse." Pivoting, Claire wandered back into the house.

David heaved a sigh of relief while he waited for her to return. A few moments later, Claire appeared with her purse in hand.

After Claire closed and locked her door, David asked, "Do you like clam chowder?"

Claire smirked. "Only if you plan on taking me to Splash Café." She followed him out to his truck. "It's the only kind I like."

"Is there anywhere else to get it?" David opened his truck door, motioning for her to climb in. "In my mind, there isn't any other place that compares."

Smiling, Claire slid into the truck. "I completely agree," she replied.

Shutting the door, David walked around to the driver's side. His heart hammered making heat smolder in his cheeks. Taking a deep breath, he willed himself to settle down. Once in control, he opened his door and climbed in, pulling it closed. Putting the keys into the ignition, David said, "I'm glad to hear you like Splash Café too."

"Mom took me and Alexis there our entire lives…" Claire's voice faded away. The lines between her eyebrows deepened and railroad tracks ran across her forehead. Exhaling, Claire glanced down at her hands in her lap, before peering out the passenger side window. "I've so many memories of walking there in the summer."

"I'm sure you do." David started the ignition. He wondered what direction to take the conversation, away from memories or allow Claire to wrangle with them. Pulling away from the curb, he asked, "What time does Alexis get home? I'll make sure to have you back by then."

Smoothing out the top of her hair, Claire replied, "Alexis texted me after you dropped me off. They ended up driving to San Luis Obispo to shop, so she won't be home until this evening, so no rush."

His shoulders loosened. "Great," smiled David. "I'm glad we can take our time."

They drove the rest of the way in contented quiet. David rolled down the windows a tad to let the salt air filter through the cab of the truck.

Abruptly, Claire spoke up with a strained voice and said, "Could you please not go this way?" She gripped the door handle with one hand, while she rubbed her other hand frantically back and forth over her thigh. "I haven't been by the convenience store… since you know…" Her voice cracked. She gripped harder onto the door handle, squeezing her eyes shut.

At first David was confused, then the reality of it crystallized in his mind. "Yes, sorry." He took the first available right turn. Only the edge of the convenience store peeked out on the other side of the light. He weaved his way over four blocks in a big loop. "I should've realized."

"I thought…" Her voice was shaky, making his middle clench tight. Pinching the bridge of her nose, she continued, "I thought I could handle it." Tears streamed down her cheeks, seeping into her shirt. "Apparently, I was wrong."

David was at a loss as to how to help. Pulling into the parking lot by the pier, David found a spot and parked the car. After turning the car off, he rested his arm along the back of truck bench. Claire swiped at the tears cascading down her cheeks. Both stared out the windshield, taking in the soothing view of the ocean and pier.

Claire leaned into his arm. David took it as an invitation to wrap his arm fully around her shoulders. "I think about it all the time." She closed her eyes for a moment, shaking her head. "Mom's last minutes of life. She ran to the convenience store to get a loaf of bread to make Alexis a sandwich for her school lunch. She told my sister she'd be right back. But she walked in, grabbed a loaf of bread… and then…" Claire's voice faded, shaking her head she stared down at her hands gripped together in her lap. David tugged Claire closer, shifting Claire rested her head on his shoulder and sobbed. "And then she was gone." Her voice was almost a whisper.

For a long time, they sat in the truck with only the sounds of the ocean filling the cab of the truck. David wanted to help, to take away the pain, but he knew it wasn't possible. Instead, David simply held Claire and didn't let go. Claire buried her head against his chest. Her sobs eventually subsided. Claire pulled away, sitting straight up. She wiped under her eyes.

"I'm sorry. I'm a mess. I thought I could handle seeing where it happened, but I guess I'm not ready. I know it was an accident. I mean the driver had a heart attack and rammed his car straight through the convenience store right into her. The driver died on the scene too. But I go over it again and again in my head. If only... if only..." Claire clasped and unclasped her hands. "I'm sorry. I don't mean to burden you with this. It isn't fair. I apologize."

It wasn't anything David didn't already know. He read about the unfortunate event in the local newspaper. Everyone in Pismo knew, the front of the convenience store was still boarded up with plywood. Apparently, the glass windows were on back order.

David pressed a finger to her lips. "Shh. Nonsense. I'm glad you can talk to me about it. I'll listen, anytime you want to talk." He removed his finger. His gaze caught hers. "I used to think about those same things all the time after Blake died. What if I had driven? What if we had left a few minutes earlier? Or what if the music hadn't been so loud? It's enough to drive you into an unhealthy never-ending cycle of what ifs. You can't do that to yourself. I know it's hard, but I would try your best to not focus on how your mom died but instead on how she lived."

After a long shaky exhale, Claire said, "She was incredible." Her voice was stronger than before. "She made everything special." Her eyes lit up, pushing out the darkness.

"I'm sure she did. I'm convinced moms have superpowers," replied David.

"I agree," said Claire.

"And Claire..." David added, "you're so strong. I'm in awe of you. Alexis is lucky to have you as a sister, even if she doesn't always show it. I know your mom would be proud of you and how you're handling everything."

"Thanks." Claire pulled down the visor, flipping open the little mirror attached to it. Taking in her image, she ran a finger under her eyes. "I think I've cried enough for today. My blotchy red face has become my signature color." She slammed the visor shut, turning to face David again.

Unbuckling his seat belt, and before David had time to think he replied, "I, for one, think you look beautiful no matter what."

"I... I..." Claire stammered, rubbing her hands back and forth rapidly over her thighs. "Thanks... you don't have to say that. I look horrible, but thank you, nonetheless."

David opened his door. "I wanted to say it..." He slipped out, turning to look back into the truck at her. "Because I mean it. You're beautiful."

Her lips twitched, finally curving up into a smile. "Thanks, David."

David closed the door, walking around to open her door. His body buzzed, sending a zing down his spine. The feeling was familiar. This wasn't the first time he'd traveled down this road, and he knew the signs.

He was falling for Claire.

CHAPTER SEVEN

"Claire, I'm home!" bellowed Alexis as she passed through the front door. "Did you miss me?"

The old wood floorboards creaked under the weight of her feet, further announcing her arrival.

"I'm in the living room!" Claire replied.

After David had dropped her off, Claire had settled onto the couch. Mindlessly, she turned on a home makeover show. Alexis appeared in the threshold between the hallway and living room.

Crossing her arms, Alexis leaned against the wall. "I'm surprised you kept the couch." Her eyes roamed over the almost empty room with a head nod toward couch, she continued, "You've sold everything that wasn't nailed down."

Claire rubbed her hand over the top of the well-worn brown leather couch. "If I thought somebody would've bought it, I would've sold it too. But it's way too old and cracked for anyone to want it." She shrugged, pushing away the years of shared memories on the very couch. Her voice cracked. "We can pull it out to the curb the day we move, and the city will pick it up and take it to the dump."

Plopping down on the empty cushion next to her, Alexis replied, "You're right about some things…" She reached over and pulled the blanket sprawled over the armrest, covering herself with it. "Nobody would pay any money for this couch. I told mom for years to replace it."

Claire ran a finger over a huge crack in the cushion. "Me too." She muted the TV Turning to face Alexis, Claire tucked her feet under herself. "I don't think Mom had the money to replace it. But it sure is comfortable."

A smile crept across Alexis's face, scanning the old couch. "I'd take comfy over nice looking any day."

"Agreed," replied Claire.

Claire then asked about her day with Juliet. Alexis lit up, explaining about the fun shops they visited.

After Alexis spoke about her day, she raised an eyebrow, "And how did things go with David?" asked Alexis. "Do you still think he's hot?" Before Claire answered, Alexis continued, "I was mad at him for not calling you after the movie, but he has redeemed himself. I mean David helped you for the whole day for free, that certainly counts for something."

Unmuting the TV Claire glanced at the screen. "He was extra helpful today." Claire didn't continue, but instead she turned up the volume of the home makeover show.

Speaking louder, over the TV "And?" Alexis whacked her on the thigh.

"And…" Claire kept her gaze forward, though she could feel the heat smearing across her cheeks and chest. "I still think he's hot, but I don't know if he's interested. I think he might simply be a nice guy helping us like he'd help anyone else he thought was in need."

"Nah…" Alexis pulled out her cell phone from her pocket. "Keep telling yourself that. I think it's a bunch of hogwash. He's into you."

Interest piqued. Claire leaned forward, pulling down Alexis's cell phone from her face. "Why do you think he's into me?"

Alexis yanked her phone from Claire's hand. "I don't know." She shrugged. "He's certainly always staring at you."

"Like how does he stare at me?" asked Claire.

"Like you're the only one in the room," said Alexis without looking up.

Claire wanted to press her for more information, to ask her to give her examples, but she knew it wouldn't be helpful. If David wanted to see her again, he'd contact her. Dropping it, they watched TV until the end of the episode.

Once it was over, Alexis stood. Stretching her arms over her head, she yawned, "I'm going to bed."

Claire flipped off the annoying infomercial for a scrambled egg microwaving device. "Me too." She stood, folding up the blanket Alexis had used, placing it back over the armrest.

Turning off the light, both left the living room.

Wandering down the hallway, Alexis stated over her shoulder, "Maybe if you and David fall in love, then we won't have to move from Pismo. We could move in with him."

Claire froze.

Blinking, Claire said, "Don't be ridiculous. I know you want to stay in Pismo, but that's not happening. Falling in love takes time. People don't rearrange their entire lives in a few short months. Sorry kiddo. In two months, we'll be gone. I need to get back to my job or we're going to run out of money."

Alexis rolled her eyes. "David's rich. He's an orthodontist. He could take care of us."

Pinching the bridge of her nose, Claire inhaled, forcing the frustration in her chest to settle. "David isn't rich."

"I'm sure he has more money than us," said Alexis.

"It isn't hard to have more money than us," replied Claire.

"I know." Alexis shook her head. "This is why you need to marry David."

"You shouldn't marry someone for their money." Claire knew it was pointless trying to explain this to a teenager. "You should marry someone, because you're in love and can't imagine life without them."

"I knew you were a romantic at heart." Alexis smirked. "Besides you've already told me multiple times about how hot you think David is, so no worries, I know you aren't after his money."

Claire groaned. Her jaw clenched. "David and I aren't getting married. Now…" She motioned toward the bedrooms. "Let's go to bed. It's been a long day."

Alexis held her hands up in defense. "No need to get all testy." Alexis complied, walking toward her bedroom. Claire turned off the lights as she trailed along behind her. Alexis droned on, "I'm just saying, it would be very convenient if you two fell in love. I'd be okay with it. You aren't getting any younger either." She stopped, her gaze sliding down Claire's frame. "You've got five years, tops, to land yourself a guy."

Claire pointed to Alexis's bedroom. "Enough. Go to bed," she hissed.

Then Alexis cackled. "Oh, look how sensitive you're being. You like him even more than I thought. You like him— *a lot*."

∽

MONDAY MORNING, CLAIRE SHOVED ALEXIS'S SANDWICH INTO a brown paper bag. She grabbed an apple out of the fruit bowl, tossing it inside before folding the top closed. "Alexis!" Claire shouted. "We need to leave or you're going to be late. I can't come up with any more excuses for the school."

Alexis rushed into the kitchen with her backpack slung over her shoulder. "Our mom died... I think they'll understand." She grabbed the paper bag Claire held outstretched to her. Then she shoved it into her backpack, zipping it closed. She adjusted the strap over her other shoulder. "We have at least a few more months to milk that."

Claire couldn't help but laugh. "If only that's how this worked." She pointed toward the front door. "Let's hit the road."

Rolling her eyes, Alexis said, "Fine."

After managing to drop Alexis off on time for school, Claire took the long route home. Picking the road which hugged the ocean, she hoped the view of the ocean would calm the staccato beat of her heart. Sadness washed over her, Claire was going to miss this town and the memories she shared here. Once she moved Alexis into her apartment in Los Angeles, she knew Pismo would be in the rear-view mirror. They wouldn't have time to visit or have a place to stay if they did decide to come back. Her former life, the one with her mom in it, was slipping through her fingertips. And she hated it.

Claire rolled down the window a tad as she stopped at the four-way stop, a block from the Old West Cinnamon Roll Shop. Her nostrils flared from the tantalizing aroma of cinnamon rolls. A line was already wrapped around the corner, but the comfort of a perfectly baked cinnamon roll led her straight into the parking lot. Without thinking, Claire climbed out of her car and joined the long line.

Slowly, the line moved forward. Her mind was elsewhere, a mix of memories from her childhood of walking there in the summer with Mom and Alexis. Claire even remembered a few good times with her dad in it, but she tried not to think about him too much if she could help it. But then her mind wandered to David. Their Saturday together only solidified her feelings for him, but after he hadn't called or texted her, she doubted he reciprocated her feelings. Regardless, she needed to thank him for his free labor.

So, when she finally arrived at the front of the line, Claire ordered an extra dozen of the cinnamon rolls to drop off at David's office. With the morning under way, Claire figured he'd be with clients, which would work perfectly, because she could leave them with Sarah at reception. The debt would be repaid in full. With the cinnamon rolls in hand, Claire left the cinnamon roll shop and drove to David's office.

Pulling into David's orthodontist parking lot, Claire found it empty which didn't feel quite right. Nevertheless, after parking, with the cinnamon rolls in hand, she wandered across the parking lot to the front door. When she went to open it, Claire found it locked. Confused, she glanced around the door and spotted the hours of the office. Apparently, since it was Monday, the office opened later than usual, not until ten-thirty.

Double checking the time on her watch, Claire groaned. The office didn't open for another half hour. "Great," she muttered under her breath. "What do I do now?"

Pausing, she peered back at her car. Maybe she could find a pen? Then she could write a note and leave the cinnamon rolls on the doorstep. With a plan, Claire veered back toward her car. The sudden sound of squealing tires made Claire jump. David's truck peeled into the parking lot. She moved out of the way of his truck, nearly tripping on the curb. This was not how she planned on this whole thing playing out. *He already saw you. You can't run away now.*

Knees shaking, Claire fumbled her way toward his truck. Smiling, David climbed out. "Claire, what are you doing here?" His eyes glided down her body, making her skin ignite. "It's so good to see you again." He shut the door and strode over to where she waited.

See. He's glad to see you. It isn't all in your head. But he didn't contact you either, so who knows what to think.

"I— I—" Claire stammered, forgetting how to communicate. Remembering why she was there; Claire shoved the box of cinnamon rolls toward him. "I brought you these, as a thank you."

His eyes lit up, smoothing out the ball of nerves bouncing around in her gut. "You didn't need to do that." David took the box from her, glancing down at the logo printed across the top of the box. "But Old West Cinnamon Rolls are my favorite."

A pause followed. Claire wrung her hands together while shuffling her feet. When he just remained silent, she took it as her cue to leave. "Well, you have a nice day. Thanks again for your help on Saturday." Her heart hammered, making her temples throb. Casting her glance away from him, Claire moved toward her car. "I'll see you around." She spoke over her shoulder.

Claire didn't know what she expected, but it wasn't that. Deep down she desired David, but David wasn't interested in her. None of this mattered, she reminded herself, because in two months she'd drive away from Pismo and never look back.

With jittery hands, Claire opened her car door, tossing her purse onto the passenger seat. Sliding inside, she couldn't get out of there fast enough. Boy, she had been foolish. Reaching to close the door, David's voice stopped her cold.

"Wait," David called out.

Claire popped her head out her car door, craning her neck to see him. David jogged over to her car with the cinnamon rolls still in his hands.

Out of breath, he gripped the corner of her door with his

free hand. "I want to take you out." His breath started to even out. He locked eyes with her as he continued, "On a real date."

Her cheeks splashed with heat. "Umm..." Claire gripped the steering wheel. "Are you sure? I know you were only being nice helping me on Saturday. You don't have to take me out."

He flashed his pearly whites, nearly blinding her. "I mean I'm not going to argue with you about that, I am a nice guy. But I did have ulterior motives when I agreed to help you. I *wanted* to spend time with you. And truth be told, the more I am with you, the more I want to be around you and get to know you better, so what do you say? Dinner, Friday night. If Alexis is around, I don't mind her tagging along, too."

Claire gnawed on her bottom lip while fiddling with her keys. "I think Alexis is going to a play with her friends at the school, so I should be free."

"Then..." David smiled widely, dissolving any moment of doubt she experienced only moments prior. "I'll see you Friday night." He released his grip from the corner of the door, taking a step backwards. Shaking the box of cinnamon rolls, he added, "Thanks again. I'll thoroughly enjoy these."

With a trembling hand, Claire waved goodbye and told him she'd see him Friday. Claire started the car and drove home, and despite the morning dew, she was warm all over.

CHAPTER EIGHT

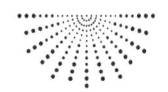

At exactly six o'clock, David arrived at Claire's house. Adjusting his jacket, he climbed out of his truck. His insides did a somersault.

After his divorce, David was left so battered and bruised, he swore off women. Then he slowly inched his way back to the land of the living, accepting invitations to dinners or blind dates. But this was different, even huge. After spending the day with Claire, David liked everything about her. He liked the way her hair fell across her shoulders, the way her eyes twinkled when she found something amusing, her wisdom and thoughtfulness, her openness about trying to piece her life together. The little snippets of time he spent with her didn't seem like enough, because try as he may, he couldn't stop thinking about her.

Wandering up to her front door, David gripped his hands into tight fists, capturing the nervous energy pulsating through his veins. Inhaling, he forced himself to relax his hands, making them hang naturally at his side. Then, with his heart in his throat, David knocked.

Twelve thumps of his heart later, the door swung open,

revealing Claire. His jaw dropped. *Dang.* Claire wore black slacks with a soft tan cashmere sweater. Her hair was curled into soft beachy waves, swinging back and forth across her shoulder blades. Trying to recover, David rubbed the back of his neck and shifted his weight. Gulping, David tried to remember how to speak.

Tilting her head to the side, Claire smiled. "David," she said. "It's good to see you."

"Claire," said David. He stood frozen in place. Throat dry, he cleared it. "You look beautiful," David stammered.

Fiddling with a strand of her hair, Claire dropped it then flipped it over her shoulder. "Thanks." Her cheeks tinged pink, making her look more adorable than David thought possible. Claire glanced down at her feet. Shifting, her eyes slowly slid up the length of his body, making his skin ignite. Her gaze bored into his, and David almost forgot to breathe. "You clean up good yourself," replied Claire.

His ears perked up. David regained a tad of confidence, squaring his shoulders. "Are you ready to go?" he asked.

"I'm ready," stated Claire.

Closing the door behind her, Claire adjusted her purse and took a few steps closer to him. The space on the porch stoop was close and intimate. His nostrils flared from a whiff of the tantalizing scent of her perfume. Half stumbling a step back, David shoved his hands into his pockets. Once he regained his balance, David took a few paces toward his truck. Claire followed.

"Thanks for agreeing to go out with me," David heard himself say, though he felt like another person was talking. His mind was still reeling from being so close to Claire.

Without hesitation, Claire replied, "I enjoy your company." Arriving at the truck, Claire stopped next to David. "Anyways, where are you taking me?" She raised an eyebrow.

"Cracked Crab. I hope you aren't allergic to shellfish." David reached for the passenger side door, then twisted back around to face Claire. His eyes dilated. "I should've asked you that before our date."

Reaching out, Claire touched him on his forearm. His skin immediately warmed from her touch, sending a tingle down the side of his body.

"I'm not allergic," Claire paused, glancing down at her outfit. "But… I fear I might have overdressed."

"No way, like I said before, you look fantastic." David swung the passenger side door open, motioning for her to get in. "And they give you those little plastic bibs."

Claire slid onto the truck bench, glancing over at him after she settled in her seat. "I know, but they also give you huge wooden mallets to crack open the crabs, and the tables are covered with paper."

Reassuringly, David added, "I promise I'll crack open everything for you if you don't want to get dirty." He gripped the corner of the door, letting himself take in the entire gorgeous sight of her. "I'll take as my personal mission to make sure you don't ruin your outfit."

"Oh, I'm not that worried about it." Claire waved it off. "I'm sure it'll be fine. I only wish I had worn something more casual."

"Would you rather we go somewhere else?" David held his breath. "I'll take you wherever you want to go. I don't care where we eat, only that I get to be with you."

Rubbing her hands back and forth over her black slacks, Claire said, "Well I can't argue with that."

David smiled, closing her door. He walked around to his side to climb in.

They drove the few blocks to Pismo's small downtown located near the pier. After parking and checking into the restaurant, they were led to a table covered with paper.

While looking over the menu, David suggested they order the big bucket for two. It was what they were famous for, a mix of shellfish and corn on the cob, which they dumped right on top of the table. Instantly, Claire agreed and closed her menu, setting it aside. A server came by a few minutes later and took their order. Both enjoyed the view from their table of the ocean and pier.

Claire sipped on her drink. "I've been here so many times." She peered out at the restaurant then back at him from across the table. "I think I have the menu memorized. How about you?"

Fiddling with the ends of his sleeves, David finally pushed them halfway up his forearms. "Oh yes, too many times to count. I mean Pismo isn't huge. There are only so many eating options, but the ones they do have are delicious."

Claire nodded. A beat of silence.

David added, "I'm surprised we've never run into each other before, with Pismo being small."

Shrugging, Claire replied, "Maybe we did, but we were strangers then."

Without thinking David said, "No way." His gaze skidded across her face, illuminated by the sunlight sneaking in through the window beside them. "I would've remembered you."

Claire slowly moistened her lips. Her cheeks reddened. "Frankly..." She gulped. "I would've remembered you too." Shifting forward, she leaned her elbow on the table, cradling her chin. "You're definitely my type."

"Ruggedly handsome?" asked David teasingly.

Claire laughed then shook her head, and said, "That's a given, but no, kind, generous, compassionate. Those qualities are more of what I'm looking for."

"Isn't that what everyone is looking for?" asked David.

"You'd think so." Claire glanced out the window. "But I

don't always think that's the case." She waved it off. "Anyways, I'm glad I met you now, not earlier."

Shifting forward, inches from her, fire filled his gut. His pulse galloped while his hands became clammy. David reminded himself to reply. "Luckily, most of life is in the timing."

Claire's posture stiffened. His words hadn't landed the way he planned. What he meant to be fun and flirtatious came out entirely wrong. The timing of her mom's death certainly wasn't good timing.

"I— I'm sorry," David stammered. He tried to backtrack. "I think that came out wrong given the circumstances of your mom's passing."

With misty eyes, Claire swiped at them. "I do believe that, most of life is in the timing. I even believe God has a hand in everything." She ran a hand over the top of her hair then swept it to the side. "It's hard though. I still don't understand the injustice of it. Mom dying…"

David reached out and grabbed her hand, letting his fingers intertwine with hers. "I'm sure it's difficult. I wish I had anything better to say."

Claire glanced out across the restaurant. "This was Mom's favorite place. We came here a lot before Alexis was born, when my dad was still in our lives. After he left, Mom didn't like coming anymore, at least not until the memory of my dad was so far gone…" Her voice faded away. "It was like he never even existed."

Giving her hand another squeeze before letting go, David said, "Maybe we can make new memories here. Ones which remind you of the good times not the bad." Shifting, David glanced out the window, watching the people on the sidewalk walk on by. He exhaled. "I used to come here with my ex-wife too." He swung his gaze back to Claire, gauging her reaction.

Pausing, Claire bit her bottom lip. "Divorced?"

David gave a slight nod.

"How long?" asked Claire.

David took a sip of his water before he answered. "Three years."

Rearranging her silverware, Claire asked, "Do you have any kids?"

"No," David shook his head. "No kids. She didn't want them, but I did. I hold out hope someday to have them. How about you?"

Claire paused, her hand lingering over her fork. "Am I divorced?"

David shook his head. "No, do you want kids?"

Smiling, Claire replied, "Yeah, I want kids. I want a whole minivan of them." With a wave of her hand, she added, "I'm not divorced by the way. I've never been married."

Their conversation was interrupted by the delivery of the food. The steaming hot bucket of crab, shrimp, mussels, and corn on the cob was dumped onto the middle of the table. A server gave them their crab cracking kits, complete with a bib, wood mallet, and metal shell cracker tool.

Claire's hands flew to her cheeks as she took in the sight of the table. "This is a ton of food." She laughed, loosening a knot he didn't know he had in his stomach. "But it looks delicious. My mouth is watering already." She tied the bib around her neck.

David mirrored her movements, doing the same. He grabbed a crab and pounded it with the wooden mallet until it cracked. Digging out the meat, he popped a piece into his mouth. "I find this part highly satisfying."

Her eyes sparkled back at him. "The aggressively hitting something with a mallet part?" Claire raised an eyebrow, picking up her mallet.

"Yes, precisely." David continued to prod the crab, digging

out the loosened meat. "Give it a try. Hitting things almost always makes anyone feel better, promise."

Claire replied with mallet in hand, "Here goes nothing." *Whack. Whack. Whack.* Claire pounded the shell of the crab. Then she burst out laughing. A sound more beautiful than anything he'd heard before. "I feel better already." Then she tugged out a piece of the exposed meat. "I need to come here more often. Just to use this mallet." Shoving the piece of crab meat into her mouth, she sighed, "It's delicious too."

"We could make it a weekly thing." David picked up his mallet again, pounding on another crab shell. "Come here and pound out all our pent-up stress."

Next, Claire picked up corn on the cob. "I like the way you think, David. I need to keep you around." Holding his gaze, she took a bite of her corn.

His heart thundered. Sweat poured down his back. Fiddling with a crab leg, he set it down and wiped his messy fingers on his napkin. David gulped. "I'd like you to keep me around too."

Claire paused mid-bite. Nodding slightly, she replied, "Then we agree, neither of us is going anywhere." After chewing and swallowing, she wiped her mouth with her napkin. "Well, at least not for another two months."

Whoosh. The mention of their dreaded timeline brought him back to reality and a list of tally marks in his mind of why things might not work between them. If he was smart and guarded his heart, tonight needed to be their first and last date. But then David glanced at Claire completely at ease and adorable, with her fingers all goopy, chowing down on corn on the cob, and his reasonable self withered away.

"I don't care." David picked up a mussel, prying open the shell. His voice became stronger as he pulled back his shoulders. "I'd rather spend the next two months with you, even if that's all I get, I'll take it. Because I like you Claire. I love the conversations we have together, and I look forward to learning more about you."

Claire grinned. "Okay then, it's settled." She swept her hair over her shoulder making the silky strands glisten from the sunlight cascading through the window. His chest pinched tight. Shifting forward, Claire continued, "Now, tell me why you wanted to become an orthodontist, because the thought of sticking my fingers into someone else's mouth makes me want to gag."

David chuckled. "Good question. Luckily it doesn't bother me one bit." He cracked another crab leg with the metal tool. "When I was a child, I listened to a guy speak at career day at my school about being a dentist. He worked with Operation Smile, and I knew right then that's what I wanted to do." He took a sip of his water then leaned closer to Claire. "I wanted to help people. Orthodontics came about in dental school. I applied and received one of the few coveted orthodontics residencies."

"Have you ever done anything with Operation Smile?" asked Claire.

Nodding, David replied, "Every chance I can. It's very rewarding." He lightly touched her on the forearm. "But believe it or not, seeing the transformation of people's smiles after braces is rewarding too. Especially in the teenagers, when they get those braces off and look at their perfect smile for the first time." He blissfully sighed. "It's incredible. I could live off that forever." He removed his hand.

"I'm glad you found something you loved." Claire shifted her body toward him, only inches apart.

They ate some more, nearly touching, but not quite. It drove him batty.

Then glancing around the table, Claire patted her stomach. "I'm stuffed. I don't think I can eat one more thing."

"Me too." David looked around the restaurant and motioned to the server.

They chatted until the server returned with their check. He couldn't remember an evening he enjoyed more. The loneliness of the past three years was whittling away. Claire was reminding him of what it was like to have someone you looked forward to seeing.

After paying, they left the Cracked Crab. The last rays of sunlight stretched across the sky. Sunset was minutes from completion. "Do you want to walk to the end of the pier?" asked David.

He didn't want the evening to end. A taste of Claire wasn't enough, he craved to be around her longer.

Claire glanced at her watch. "Sure. I need to be home in an hour. I don't want Alexis to beat me home."

"I'll get you home on time," stated David. "I promise."

Hiking up her purse on her shoulder, Claire nodded, turning toward the pier. David reached out, interlacing his fingers with hers. She didn't move away but drew her body closer to his, gripping onto the crook of his elbow with her other hand. Her nearness sent a zing down his back. Breathing in her sweet intoxicating scent, fire raged in his gut.

In a haze, David walked hand and hand with Claire to the end of the pier. When they arrived at the very end, David let go of her hand leaning over the wooden railing, glancing out at breathtaking view. The water glistened with the tiny bit of sunlight. Rhythmic sounds of the ocean waves sounded in his ears. Claire came up next to him, touching her shoulder to his own. She ran her hands over the rough surface of the pier railing.

Both stood watching until the sun completely disappeared, trading the sun for the moonlight and a smattering of stars. It was breathtakingly beautiful, and

David appreciated Claire next to him, enjoying and appreciating the view too.

"I'm going to miss it here," said Claire. Staring out to the vast ocean, Claire's shoulders stooped. "I've missed this place every day since I moved away to Los Angeles. I didn't realize how much until being here these last weeks." She gnawed on her bottom lip. "I wish there was a way I could stay here. For Alexis."

Wrapping his arm around her shoulders, David pulled Claire closer to his body. Mirroring his movements, Claire wrapped an arm around his waist, keeping her gaze at the ocean.

"Alexis is lucky to have you." His words failed him. David didn't know how to make the situation better. Claire didn't have enough money to stay. Her job and life were in Los Angeles. Somehow, he wished he magically had the ability to fix it for her.

Glancing up at the dark sky, the stars twinkled back at him. David cleared his throat, "What about you? You say you've missed Pismo since you moved away." David shifted, leaning his back against the wood railing to face Claire. "Would you ever live here permanently, for you?"

Claire's hair flew in every direction. Without thinking David reached out, tucking her wisps of hair behind her ear. His hand lingered, cupping her neck. Claire took a step closer, standing between his legs, making him all too aware of the warmth of her body. Claire inhaled. Silence followed, so wide and so vast, it made his temples pulsate. The air between them crackled and sizzled. Her hand found his chest, and she laid her palm flat against it. He tugged her closer, wrapping his arm around her waist bringing them hip to hip.

Tilting her chin up, Claire whispered, "Maybe, if I had

someone to stay for. I would stay. Especially if it was someone like you."

David ran his thumb down the length of her jaw. Her skin was smooth and silky against the pad of his finger. He unconsciously licked his lips. "How about if it was me? In a perfect world, I'd want to be here in Pismo with you." His gaze bore into hers. Waiting for her to indicate, she was feeling the same heat building between them.

Claire stood on her tiptoes, bringing her face closer to his. David didn't hesitate. It was all the invitation he needed. Crossing the mere inch between them, he made his lips collide with hers. Immediately, Claire melted against him, running a finger along his collar bone. Her fingertips tucked around the collar of his shirt. His insides did a somersault, making his pulse triple its speed. The worries of the future faded away, because in the here and now, David was kissing Claire. And he never wanted it to end. He tugged her closer, tightening his grip around her waist, supporting her.

As her lips danced with his, David remembered again what it was like to have someone, someone who made the little pieces of your life fit back together, so you felt complete. He remembered how hope could feel, because for the first time in who knew how long, he hoped for the possibility of something—someone.

Since his divorce, David hadn't allowed himself to believe in anything. Instead, he put a cage around his heart and declared love never lasted, people never stayed, and maybe he was better off alone. But kissing Claire, holding her, David's prior arguments no longer held their shape. The constant dull ache in his heart, his steady companion for the past few years, fluttered away with the ocean breeze.

Brushing his tongue along her bottom lip, he tasted the fruity tang of her lip balm. Inhaling her scent, his nostrils flared, while his skin ignited. He wondered how kissing someone could feel this right, feel this perfect.

Finally, David forced himself to pull away. Gasping for air, his hand flew to his exploding chest. His chest heaved as he waited to regain control. Kissing Claire on the temple, David wrapped his arms around her, bringing her tight against his chest. Claire mirrored his movements, resting her head in the crook of his neck.

"I— I—" David chuckled. Half delirious. "I don't even know what to say."

He felt Claire smile against his chest. "Please don't say anything." She loosened their embrace a tad, enough to peer up at him. With a sly smile, Claire said, "Why don't you just kiss me again?"

So he did.

CHAPTER NINE

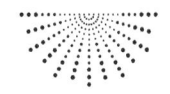

"Are you coming to my dance recital Friday night?" asked Alexis.

Claire locked the front door to the house then motioned for Alexis to start toward the car. Claire followed behind her to the driveway. "I wouldn't miss it for the world. Why would you think I wouldn't come?"

Alexis shrugged. "I was only worried you made plans with David."

"Nothing is more important than going to your dance recital," replied Claire. "I know how hard you've been working at your practices."

At the car, Claire opened the door, settling into her seat.

Alexis climbed in next to her, shoving her backpack between her feet. "I was only checking. You've been walking around in a little love bubble haze since you guys officially started dating."

Starting the car, Claire backed out of the driveway. "I have not."

"Yes, you have." Alexis buckled her seatbelt. "It's kind of

cute. I've never seen you like this, not even when you were dating that one guy..." Alexis squinted her eyes then snapped. "Theo, the radiologist."

Claire groaned. "Please don't remind me." Theo and she had met at the hospital she worked at. He wasn't anyone to write home about, but unfortunately it took Claire a while to figure it out. Theo still worked there too, but Claire skillfully avoided him. "I've been trying to forget about him."

"He was the worst." Alexis groaned. "Theo talked about himself nonstop. *I'm the best, blah blah blah.* It was so annoying." She shook her head and sighed. "I can't believe you thought you loved him."

"I know, but I was young." Claire made a right-hand turn. "I had no idea what love even felt like, but now I know I didn't ever love Theo. I was only flattered he showed interest in me. In the beginning, Theo was very charming, but then eventually his true colors came out."

"I'm glad you kicked him to the curb." Alexis tsked. "But it took you *so* long to figure out he was no good."

Defensively, Claire replied, "We only dated for six months."

"Six months too long." Alexis paused then waved a hand. "Enough about Theo. Who cares?" she paused then added, "I don't mind if you want to invite David to my recital on Saturday night."

"What? Invite David?" Claire stopped at the light, glancing over at Alexis. "I'm sure he already has plans." Though Claire doubted it. They had spent every available minute together since their kiss on the pier. David stopped by after work every night, to eat dinner and hang out with her and Alexis.

"Doubtful," Alexis smirked. "The guy has nothing going on. That's why he's always at our house. I don't mind. I like him. He's fun and has helped you not be so sad since Mom died. I *want* you to invite David."

"I don't know if ballet is David's thing." Claire turned into the school parking lot. She didn't know why she was hesitant to invite David to the recital.

"You are so dense sometimes." Alexis rolled her eyes. "The ballet isn't the point. If David is into you, he won't care where he's going only that you're there too."

Staring over at Alexis, Claire asked, "How old are you again?"

Alexis opened her door. "Thirteen." She hopped out, pivoting back around. "But apparently I know more about guys than you do." Then she shut the door, wandering into the school.

Shaking her head, Claire pulled out of the school parking lot. She wondered when Alexis had become an expert on relationships. To her knowledge Alexis hadn't even held a guy's hand. Her words planted some ideas into Claire's head. Maybe extending an invitation for David to attend Alexis's recital wasn't a bad idea. Truth was, David needed to know that Alexis and she were a package deal. He couldn't have one without the other.

Claire didn't have time to worry too much about her conversation with Alexis, because as she pulled into her driveway, her phone rang. Her Bluetooth flashed the number on her car's dashboard, making her heart sink. The sound of the ring vibrated again in the car.

Taking a deep breath, Claire hit accept on the dashboard. "Hello, this is Claire." She turned off the engine but remained seated.

"Claire, I'm glad I was able to catch you. This is Mr. Howard from the cemetery. I've tried calling a few times, but I haven't been able to speak to you directly." He paused.

Claire pinched the bridge of her nose. "I know… sorry

about that." Closing her eyes for a moment, Claire attempted to find her equilibrium. "But you have me now. What can I do for you today?"

"Like I mentioned at the burial, we need you to finalize the inscription for your mom's headstone. Were you able to decide?" asked Mr. Howard.

Skillfully, Claire had avoided this decision for the last several weeks. Once the inscription was done, then everything would be final. And Claire hadn't been ready to unpack what that meant.

Claire cleared her throat, "What is the remaining balance again?"

"Let me double check. Would this be with the inscription you gave me earlier. Or did you want to make some changes?"

Honestly, Claire couldn't remember what she wrote down in a grief-stricken haze. How did she sum up the one person in her life that meant everything to her? Nothing seemed sufficient.

"Could you remind me of the inscription? I can't remember," asked Claire.

Claire heard him shuffle some papers around.

"I have it right here." Mr. Howard cleared his throat. "It will read 'A mother's love, like an imperishable sun, cannot go out.' Are you still okay with that inscription?"

"Sure," Claire ran a hand over the top of her hair.

"So, with no additional changes, the balance due will be $1,752," stated Mr. Howard.

Claire slumped in her seat. She knew headstones were costly, but she didn't realize how expensive they were. If she chose a different one, she would start the entire awful process over again.

A pinch between her shoulder blades made her neck ache. "When is the balance due?" asked Claire.

"We need the balance to start the headstone inscription. That's why I'm calling. We can't risk getting stuck with something someone can't pay for. Unfortunately, this happens a lot in our business," replied Mr. Howard.

"I understand." Claire locked her jaw. "I'll bring by a check as soon as possible."

Claire ended the call. Throwing her head into her palmed hands, Claire didn't know how she'd pay for it. After selling off most of Mom's things, she saved some funds, but it was needed for their move to Los Angeles. Putting the headstone on a credit card was an option, but Claire had never taken on debt. Mom had insisted that Claire should live within her means, and to only purchase things when they could be paid for in full.

With no solution, Claire climbed out of the car and went inside. She walked slowly through the almost empty home. Each room only contained a few stray items. There was nothing of any real value left to sell. Even if she wanted to, it wouldn't be enough to cover the headstone and the necessary move.

Stressed out, Claire settled at Mom's desk, a family heirloom from her great grandmother, the one piece of furniture Claire refused to sell. The top of the desk was covered with different bills, bills which needed to be paid. Her heart raced and anxiety pulsated through her, and instead of leaning into the panic, she whispered a silent prayer. God always found a way. She only wondered how He'd help her this time.

Then her gaze landed on a box Claire had placed on the desk weeks ago. Slowly, she peeled back the closed top. Inside were dozens of condolence cards collected at the funeral. In her grief, Claire failed to open any of them. Taking the first one out of the box, she ran her finger under the seal to open it and out dropped forty dollars. She gasped.

Surely, it was the only card containing money. After reading the kind message, Claire picked up another card and opened it, revealing another twenty dollars.

Claire spent the rest of the morning reading and opening the cards. She cried as she read the sweet words of encouragement, many from people she didn't know. Some were former students Mom had taught over the years. Many commented on how Mom was their favorite teacher and retold memories of their experience in her class. When every card was opened, Claire counted the money, it was sufficient to cover the cost of the headstone. Claire wept, thankful for the kindness of others.

Then her phone dinged. Claire fished it out of her pocket, revealing a message from David.

> I hope your day is going well. Can I come by tonight? I'd love to see you again. I'll bring dinner for you and Alexis.

> Sounds great! Maybe 6?

> Great, see you then.

Smiling, Claire slid her phone back into her pocket. Her mood was lighter than only hours earlier. Gathering up the money, Claire left to pay for the headstone before picking up Alexis from school.

Later that evening, Alexis sat at the kitchen table finishing up some homework. "What time is David going to be here? I'm starving." She slammed her pencil down on top of her spiral notebook.

"I told him six." Claire glanced over at her from her place in the kitchen. She was sorting through the cupboards, still deciding what to get rid of and what to keep. "He should be here any minute."

She placed some more of the random unnecessary kitchen items into a box to be donated. Mom had been a wonderful cook, but Claire had no use for twenty spatulas. The kitchen in her apartment was tiny and was already stocked with what she needed.

Groaning, Alexis face planted herself on top of her open textbook. "I hope he doesn't bring something I don't like."

Claire went to the kitchen sink to wash her hands. Over her shoulder, she said, "I think you'll like what he brings. David specifically asked about what you liked, and I gave him some suggestions."

Alexis perked up, sitting straight again. "He did?" She smiled. "I knew I liked him."

Turning back around, Claire finished washing her hands. She dried them on the towel hanging from the oven handle. "I'm glad." Her own stomach rumbled. "David's thoughtful like that. I still can't believe he's divorced. I mean who divorces a guy who asks about food preferences?"

Waving her pencil at her, Alexis said, "Someone who doesn't appreciate how good she has it."

Claire nodded, silently agreeing.

Alexis added, "But her loss is your gain."

Before Claire commented, the doorbell rang. "He's here." Claire smiled, walking toward the door. "I'll get it."

"Just make sure you do any kissing out of my sight," yelled Alexis. "I don't need that image burned into my brain."

With a chuckle, Claire rolled her eyes. Walking the remaining distance to the door, Claire opened it, revealing David on the stoop.

With hands full of food, David grinned, melting her middle into a gooey mess. "Hey, beautiful," he leaned in and kissed her on the cheek. Claire held open the door for David to enter. He passed through the door. "I hope I've got enough food."

"I'm sure whatever you brought will be great." Claire closed the door behind David, then she motioned for him to follow her into the kitchen.

Arriving in the kitchen, David set the food on top of the kitchen counter. From her spot at the table, Alexis eyed the bags.

"Hi, Alexis." David unpacked several boxes of food. "Claire told me Chinese food was your favorite."

Alexis closed her textbook, placing it and her notebook into her backpack. Standing, she strode across the kitchen, joining them. Peering over the food, Alexis said, "As long as you have orange chicken and chow mein, then I'll be fine."

David grabbed two cartons marked as orange chicken and chow mein respectively. "Here, these are just for you." He held them out to her.

Taking the cartons from him, Alexis smiled warmly. "Thanks, can I keep the leftovers for tomorrow?"

"Of course," replied David.

"Great," Alexis nudged Claire with her shoulder. "You should see the stuff Claire tries to feed me."

"Ha. Ha. You're hilarious." Claire sighed. "You're lucky I don't let you starve. I've never claimed to be a good cook."

With food in hand, Alexis slumped into her chair at the table, placing the food in front of herself. Blankly, Alexis stared at the boxes of food. "No..." She sighed, making her shoulders noticeably droop. Her eyes became misty, and she swiped the moisture away with her index finger. "Mom was the cook."

Claire gripped the end of the counter with her hands as the room spiraled around her. Lungs burning, she gasped for air. Grief was tricky. One moment you were fine, then the next you couldn't breathe. Blinking rapidly, Claire fought hard against the floodgate starting to break. Someday, she hoped it wasn't this difficult, wished she could remember Mom without overwhelming, debilitating sadness.

Forcing herself to find her equilibrium, Claire finally said, "Mom was the best cook." Her voice cracked as a few tears ran down her cheeks.

Glancing out the kitchen window, Claire remembered Mom cooking in this very kitchen too many times to count. Some meals were made on a shoestring budget, other times Mom managed to find nice cuts of meat at discount prices at the supermarket, and her concoctions were closer to what a gourmet chef served in the very finest restaurants. Mom spent hours cooking for her and Alexis, a labor of love, Claire didn't fully appreciate the act until this moment.

David's voice broke the stillness. "What's your favorite dish that your mom made?" He leaned against the counter, folding his arms, and crossing his ankles.

Claire shifted toward David, locking eyes with him. Gratitude seeped into her entire being. How did he manage to pivot everything back to positivity? It was a quality Claire loved in him.

Thank you, Claire mouthed to David. Then Claire glanced at Alexis, wondering if Alexis wanted to share first.

A smile spread across Alexis's face. "I loved her chicken enchiladas." Alexis swiped at her eyes with the back of her palm. "Or her garlic pesto chicken."

"You had me at enchiladas," replied David. Grabbing the rest of the bags of food, he walked them to the table and sat in the seat across from Alexis. Opening a carton of fried rice, David continued, "Did she ever teach you how to make her enchiladas?"

Following suit, Claire grabbed some forks and plates before joining Alexis and David at the table. Alexis opened her orange chicken, filling the room with its tantalizing aroma. Claire's stomach rumbled as Alexis spooned the food onto her plate.

"You know Mom and I made them once together," remarked Alexis. Spearing a piece of her orange chicken, Alexis continued, "but I wouldn't remember how to make them now."

Claire opened a carton of broccoli beef, putting some onto her plate before handing the carton to David. David handed her the spicy shrimp in return.

"I'm pretty decent at reading a recipe." David speared a piece of beef and took a bite. After swallowing, he said, "I'd love to learn how to make enchiladas. Maybe we could do it together, Alexis?"

Shifting in her seat, Alexis's gaze darted quickly between Claire and David. "Wouldn't you want to do that with Claire?"

David nudged Claire with his shoulder. "No, you already told me she can't cook."

"Hey..." Claire suddenly felt defensive even though she couldn't argue. "I could maybe try."

Wrapping an arm around Claire's shoulders, David kissed her on the temple. "It's okay you can't cook. You have lots of other wonderful qualities. Besides, I was asking *Alexis* if she wanted to take a crack at the recipe with me."

Alexis smirked. "I'd like that, David." She leaned across the table and looked at Claire. "Have you already packed up Mom's cookbooks?"

Claire shook her head. "No. I haven't gotten to it yet." She served herself some of the chow mein then took a bite. "That was the next cupboard I was going to tackle."

Jumping up, Alexis went to the cupboard where Mom kept her cookbooks. She rummaged through a few of them until she found the one she wanted. Enthusiastically, Alexis held it up and tapped the cover with her index finger. "I remember this is the cookbook with the recipe in it." Alexis brought it back to the table, putting it down on the table next to her.

David finished chewing, then said, "If you make a list of the ingredients, then we can go shopping together to get everything we need to make them."

"Can I come too?" asked Claire.

Claire appreciated David taking an interest in Alexis, but she didn't want to be left out.

"No," replied Alexis. "You weren't invited."

David patted Claire's thigh. "Sorry, Claire." He took another bite of the broccoli beef. "You heard the boss." David made a head tilt toward Alexis.

Claire scoffed. "Why can't I come, Alexis?" Folding her arms against her body, she acted more hurt than she felt.

"Because..." Alexis rolled her eyes. "You'll just try and take over, and then I'll never learn."

"Geez, please don't hold back on how you really feel," replied Claire.

Smugly, Alexis said, "I won't."

Claire's shoulders drooped, embarrassed Alexis found it imperative to point out to David she was both a bad cook and needed to be in control. Two big strikes against her. If she kept going, Alexis might manage to scare David away.

David leaned in closer to Claire. His breath tickled her neck as he cupped her ear and whispered. "Claire, don't you worry, I like you just the way you are." His hand slid away from her ear, down the length of her arm, smoothing out the knot in between her shoulder blades. "This is going to be our project." David winked at Claire. "We promise you can eat the finished product. Right, Alexis?" He glanced at Alexis with a raised eyebrow.

"Yep." Alexis nodded. "We'll make dinner. You won't have to do a thing. You deserve a break."

Leaning back in her chair, Claire folded her arms. "Do I?"

"Yes, you do." David fiddled with her hair, swiping it over her shoulder. "Alexis and I have this."

Her skin tingled. Claire threw up her hands. "Fine. You'll make dinner, and I'll eat it."

"See," Alexis said. "You can't say I don't do anything for you."

Claire laughed. "Touché."

CHAPTER TEN

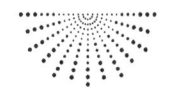

David entered his parents' house, and Jasper ran down the hallway to greet him. Scooping Jasper up, David wandered down the hallway in the direction of the sound of his parents' TV "Mom, Dad, are you back there?" David stroked Jasper between his ears.

"Shh," Kelly bellowed. "We're watching Survivor."

He chuckled to himself. His parents' obsession with the show was unlike anything he had otherwise witnessed. Quietly, David continued into the living room. His parents were cuddled up on the couch, David plopped down on the empty loveseat. Attention glued to the TV, neither glanced over at him. Jasper settled onto his lap, and David rubbed his fur in long methodical strokes until Jasper fell asleep.

Finally, Survivor went to a commercial. Kelly hit the pause button on the DVR device. David gasped. "You're recording this? Why didn't you pause it when I came in?"

"You know we only pause it during commercials, so we can fast forward through them." Stephen adjusted the blanket spread haphazardly across both his and Kelly's laps. He raised an eyebrow. "Did you stop by for a reason? You never come by when we're watching Survivor."

Kelly threw the blanket off her lap, grabbing an empty popcorn bowl. "You have five minutes before we turn it back on." Wiggling off the couch, she walked to the kitchen and placed it in the sink. "Hey, how did helping Claire and Alexis with the garage sale go? I never asked."

David paused mid-stroke, moving a sleeping Jasper on the cushion next to him. "Good." He glanced over at his parents, wondering if he should tell them more. Like how Claire was both fascinating and intriguing. Like how she managed to fill a void in his life he didn't really know was there until now. David leaned forward, resting his elbows on his thighs and steepled his hands together. "Claire and I've been hanging out a lot since then."

"Is that right?" Stephen folded his arms. "And by hanging out do you mean helping her out or dating?"

Returning to her seat next to Stephen, Kelly readjusted the blanket over her lap. "David..." Her voice was pointed. "Please tell me you didn't kiss her already." She tilted her head to the side, studying him.

David shifted, gripping both sides of the couch cushion. "I like Claire. I think there might be something there." His gaze darted between his parents, judging their reaction.

Kelly shook her head. "David, this isn't a good idea. Claire just lost her mom. And she's moving soon. It won't work." She wagged her finger at him. "And I know how you love a project and love to be the hero."

"It isn't like that." David ran a hand down the length of his face. "I know none of it makes sense, but I enjoy being with Claire, and Alexis too. And it's too late, I like her, and I've already kissed her."

Stephen smirked.

Kelly threw up her hand. "I asked you to help her with a garage sale, not date her," she groaned.

"I thought you liked Claire." David stated, pointing at Kelly. "You practically pushed me onto her when you volunteered for me to spend a whole Saturday with her. What did you expect?"

Kelly threw down both of her hands on top of the blanket. "I don't know." She shook her head. "Not this." Then she glanced at her watch. "Your five minutes are up. We'll have to talk about this later. I worry about you getting hurt. They're moving, and you're not." She folded her arms.

"Be careful David." Stephen picked up the remote and fast forwarded through the commercials, cuing it to the correct spot. "Claire and Alexis will be gone soon. It's probably best to not start anything." Then he turned the TV back on.

"It's too late," muttered David under his breath. "I couldn't back out now if I wanted to."

If only they knew, Claire already had him wrapped around her finger. And Alexis only sweetened the deal. David regretted stopping by his parents' house. Naïvely, David thought they would be happy for him. Because for the first time in however long, David was optimistic about his future. The last few years of being alone—well, lonely—weren't ones he wanted to repeat. Claire and Alexis had brightened his life in a way he didn't know he needed. So, though it wasn't wise, David didn't care. He planned on leaning into the feeling of happiness, even if it eventually blew up in his face.

∽

SLOWLY, PUSHING THE CART DOWN THE AISLE, DAVID STOPPED in front of the endcap with shelves of tortillas. "What kind of tortillas do we need? Flour or corn?" He shifted his weight, glancing over at Alexis.

Alexis peered down at her list of ingredients. Her finger ran across the paper. "It doesn't say." She groaned. Pinching the bridge of her nose, she finally said, "My gut tells me we need to buy corn tortillas."

David grabbed a pack of the corn tortillas off the shelf, tossing it into the cart. "Let's go with your gut. Isn't that what every expert chef says?"

Alexis laughed. Her demeanor softening. "I, personally, don't know any expert chefs. Do you?"

David tipped up the bill of his baseball cap a tad. "No, but it's on those cooking shows." He wandered further down the aisle. "They tell you to work with what you have."

"You watch cooking shows?" Alexis's eyes widened while she trailed along beside him. "Why? You said you don't cook."

"I watch it more to see the creative process. I like the one where they have to cook something with a secret ingredient." Pausing, David stopped in the middle of the aisle. "I've no clue what the show is called or why I like it so much."

Putting a hand to her chest, Alexis replied, "Please don't look at me," she shook her head. "I don't know how to psychoanalyze that. I'm a teenager."

David laughed. The subject was dropped.

"Ahh, okay, let's see." Alexis peered down at her list again. "Next, we need shredded cheese." She groaned as she double checked the list, then she tilted it in David's direction for him to see. "Again, it doesn't say what kind." Her shoulders drooped. Running a hand through her hair, Alexis added, "These are going to turn out horrible. I see why Claire can't cook. This is harder than I thought." Her eyes started to mist. "Mom always knew what to buy. She would literally get the shopping done in ten minutes flat. I'd just wander along behind her while she grabbed everything, she needed without even stopping the cart."

David readjusted his baseball cap. "I'm sure she was good

at it." Wrapping an arm around Alexis's shoulder, he lowered his voice, "But we'll get better at this too. Promise. If we mess these up, because we get the ingredients all wrong, we can try again next week. It's no big deal." He gave her shoulders a slight squeeze before letting go.

"I guess you're right." Alexis grabbed a pack of random cheese and placed it in the cart.

They continued down the ethnic food aisle, stopping in front of rows of enchilada sauce.

Clearly losing her steam, Alexis grabbed a random type of enchilada sauce without even double checking and tossed it into the cart. David wanted to make sure they were covered so he grabbed two different types too and added them to the cart.

"I don't know why I'm putting so much pressure on myself for these enchiladas to turn out..." Her voice trailed off, and Alexis stared directly in front of her. Biting her quivering bottom lip, Alexis dragged her feet slowly down the aisle. David slowed his speed to match her steps, wondering if he should jump in with another word of encouragement or allow her time to process everything. Alexis cleared her throat then finally said, "Maybe it's because if I get them right then it's one more thing I can manage to do without Mom. Like if I can make these, then all the other little things that pop up will be manageable too. I worry too though as I manage things without her eventually, I'll forget her altogether."

"No," David shook his head. "Impossible. Your mom will always be a part of you. Though I get why you are feeling discouraged, you have to remember half of life is messing up and trying again until you get it right."

"Is that how you feel about your divorce?" asked Alexis. "Do you want to try again? You know, get married."

Her question stopped him in his place. Sweat started to gather in the small of his back. "I—" David stammered. "I—"

Alexis shrugged. "Claire told me you were divorced."

"I am." David pushed the cart forward, mainly to avoid looking at Alexis directly. "I made a mistake. I'm learning to move on from it. I guess that's part of my life. I messed up, and I'm trying to make things right again."

Alexis ran her hand along the cans of vegetables as they walked toward the checkout. "You'll get it right this time around." She shrugged. "You probably just didn't pick the right person. I think marriage number two for you will be better."

"I sure hope so," said David. "It can't be worse than marriage number one."

"If you married my sister," Alexis paused, staring directly at David, "you'd get it right. She's the best person I know. Even if I grumble and give her a hard time. I know she'll always be there for me."

David's back stiffened at the mention of marrying Claire. Marriage? He wasn't anywhere close to entertaining those thoughts. He sure hoped Claire wasn't either because they had only just begun dating.

His throat grew tight. David gulped. "Claire is amazing. I can't argue with you there."

With a huge grin, Alexis replied, "She's the best, but don't tell her I said that. I don't want it going to her head."

David made a crossing motion over his heart.

They joined the checkout line. With Alexis's help, they loaded the ingredients onto the conveyor belt. David was grateful for something to occupy his hands and mind. After purchasing everything, they drove back to her house.

When they arrived, Claire came out and helped them carry the groceries inside. After unpacking the contents onto the kitchen counter, David kindly walked Claire out of the kitchen.

"Please," Claire pleaded, "can't I sit here and watch? I promise not to get in the way."

David wanted nothing more than to be near Claire, but this wasn't up to him. This project was something for him and Alexis to bond over. Glancing over his shoulder into the kitchen, David said loud enough for Alexis to hear. "It's up to the cook." He raised an eyebrow. "What do you think Alexis? Do we kick her out or let her stay?"

Opening the spice cupboard, Alexis shook her head. "Kick her out." Her voice softened a tad. "David and I wanted to make you dinner. Sometimes you need to let people do nice things for you."

David smirked. "You heard the woman." Kissing Claire on the cheek, he put both hands on her shoulders and turned her toward the hallway. "You look beautiful by the way, but sorry, I have to kick you out."

Claire made a pouty face. "I can't believe this." Fiddling with her hair, Claire finally whipped it over her shoulder. The strands cascaded down her back.

David's stomach pooled with warmth. "Go relax." David hugged her. "I promise I'll come find you once we put the food in the oven. Then we can all watch a show together while they bake."

Claire rolled her eyes. "Fine," she released their embrace, "see you soon." Then she wandered out of the kitchen.

Alexis rubbed her hands together. "I thought she'd never leave." Then she peered at the ingredients lined up on the counter and put a hand on her hip. "Now what?"

David chuckled then slapped his hand across the slick, cool countertop. "I have absolutely no idea."

Alexis's eyes dilated. "What are we going to do? I kicked

Claire out of the kitchen because I thought we had this." She gnawed on a fingernail. "I was obviously so wrong."

Then David held up his pointer finger. "We do have this. That's what a recipe is for, right?"

"Let's hope." Alexis grabbed the cookbook off the counter, opening it to the correct page.

After poring over the instructions, David and Alexis started cooking the chicken over the stovetop. Multiple times, David rechecked the next steps of the recipe. They fumbled their way through it and somehow managed to get the enchiladas into the Pyrex pan.

Before putting them into the oven, Alexis glanced down at the pan. "These don't look anything like Mom's." Her shoulders drooped. "They look awful."

"But maybe, they'll taste like them," replied David.

"I'm not holding out any hope." Alexis opened the oven, placing the enchiladas inside. She started the timer.

"I have faith they're going to be delicious," said David with a tad too much enthusiasm.

After they finished cleaning up the kitchen and setting the table, David wandered through the house looking for Claire. He called out her name a few times.

"In here!" Claire bellowed.

David followed the sound of her voice, finding her in a room which he assumed was an office. The room was practically empty. Only a desk and some packed boxes remained. Claire sat at the desk, typing on a laptop.

Claire glanced up at his arrival and stopped typing. "Are you done already?" Shifting in her seat, she stretched.

"We certainly weren't fast." David sat down on the corner of the desk, inches away from Claire. "It took us over an hour." He reached out and ran a hand down the length of her arm.

Claire double checked the clock on her laptop. "I told you

cooking wasn't easy." She leaned forward in her swivel chair. "Do you think you and Alexis have a future in cooking?"

Shaking his head, David replied, "Not a chance. But," he held up a finger, "I was happy to spend time with Alexis. It gave me an opportunity to get to know her better. She is a great kid." He couldn't help but smile.

"I know. I'm lucky to have her, even with the extra responsibilities..." Her voice trailed off, and Claire stared out the window overlooking the side yard. Methodically, she ran her hands back and forth over the armrests. "I don't know what I'd do if I didn't have her."

After a long pause, Claire swung her gaze back to him, and it almost unhinged him. Deep worry wrinkles stretched across her forehead and a sadness shone in her eyes. David knew the burden she carried was heavy, and he wanted nothing more than to wrap his arms around her and reassure her everything would be okay. But he couldn't promise her that. Nobody could.

Claire continued, "It's not like I have extra family in my life. My dad took off, and my grandparents are long gone. It's only me and Alexis. She has kept me going." Her voice cracked.

David realized how incredibly lucky he was to still have both of his parents in his life. A blessing he hadn't recognized in a while. "I'm sure glad you have each other. Alexis loves you, even if she doesn't always say it." David reached out, covering his hand over hers. Then he yanked her up and toward him, wrapping his arms around her. He whispered into her hair, "Alexis told me at the store today she needed to not be so hard on you."

Rapidly, Claire loosened their embrace enough to glance up at him. "She did?" She lowered her voice, "I don't know how to get her to talk to me. You have a way with her. I wish she'd tell me more."

Reaching out, David tucked a few of Claire's stray hairs behind her ear. He cupped her neck. "She will. Eventually, she'll probably tell you more than you want to know. Just give her a little bit of time. I'm an impartial party. Sometimes it's easier to talk to an outsider than someone you know and love."

Placing her arms around his waist, Claire gazed up at him. "You aren't an outsider to me." She quickly kissed him on the lips. "You belong right here with me."

Grinning, David touched his forehead to hers. They stared at each other for a moment too long. His heart hammered. A fire raged in his gut. David gulped. How did this woman manage to create this reaction in him in such a short amount of time?

"Thanks for coming and cooking me dinner," said Claire, breaking the silence.

With one finger, David swiped Claire's hair over her shoulder, letting his fingertips run through the silky strands. Whispering into her ear, "Alexis practically did everything. But it's our secret." Kissing her cheek, David, for a speck of time, allowed himself to imagine his life with her. Imagine a world where they could be together, forever. He hadn't dreamed in a long time, and he knew allowing himself to hope was a dangerous path to walk down. With a casual shrug, he added, "I just the read the steps off to Alexis from the recipe."

Smirking, Claire replied, "Liar. I don't believe you for a second."

David wanted to kiss her twitching lips.

From the door threshold, Alexis loudly said, "Geez, you two."

They both flinched, jumping a few inches apart and releasing one another's embrace.

Leaning one shoulder against the doorway, Alexis

continued, "Every time I stumble upon you guys, you've got your hands all over each other."

"Calm down," Claire fiddled with the ends of her shirt then pushed up her chin. "We weren't doing anything that couldn't be seen."

"Says who?" Alexis raised an eyebrow. Then Alexis shook her head, pushing off the door frame, pivoting to leave. Over her shoulder, she added, "The food's ready. Let's eat." Alexis wandered down the hall, leaving them alone.

Squeezing Claire's hand, David motioned with a head tilt toward the kitchen. "You heard Alexis, we better get in there before she reports us to who knows who."

Claire quickly gave him a peck on his lips. "Let's go eat these enchiladas you've been slaving over."

CHAPTER ELEVEN

Gasping, Claire stared down at the bubbling pan of enchiladas on the stovetop. She clasped her hands together. "These look exactly like Mom's." And they smelled as delicious as she remembered. A flood of happy memories of Mom in the kitchen cooking popped back into her mind. Her eyes misted. Claire cleared her throat, peering up at Alexis and David with a teary-eyed smile. "You both did a great job. I can't wait to try them."

"Maybe hold your praises until you eat one." Alexis carried the pan to the table, setting it on a hot pad in the center of the table. "We still aren't positive if we used the right tortillas or cheese."

"Nonsense." Claire went to the table, sitting down. David joined her, sliding into the seat next to her. Alexis sat across from them. "I think they might have turned out even better than Mom's."

"Impossible," Alexis stated. "Mom's will always be the best."

Alexis used a spatula to scoop out an enchilada for each of them, placing one onto their plates.

Picking up her fork, Claire dug into her enchiladas. Claire hoped for Alexis's sake they turned out. She took a bite, allowing the rich tangy sauce along with the meat and cheese to hit her taste buds. It melted in her mouth. Sighing, Claire said, "Mm." She pointed to her mouth. "These taste exactly like Mom's."

Wiping her face with a napkin, Alexis replied, "I agree. These taste like how I remember." She took another bite of her enchilada before she continued, "I can't believe it."

"High five." David held his flat palm up. Alexis high fived him. "I knew you could do it."

Still smiling, Alexis declared, "We did it!"

They ate in contentment until their bellies were full of the deliciousness of homemade enchiladas.

Once done, Alexis pushed out her chair. "I need to get my homework done." Standing, she grabbed her plate. "The cooking ate up my entire evening."

Waving her off, Claire said, "Go. I'll clean up. It's the least I can do."

With a slight spring in her step, Alexis placed her dirty plate in the sink then left.

David stretched then patted his belly. "I might need to get more into this cooking thing. I'm better at this than I thought."

Laughing, Claire replied, "Hey, it can't be denied. You're a talented cook. Please don't let it go to your head. I don't need you getting extra cocky about it." Claire grabbed her plate and stood, taking it to the sink. David gathered up his plate and the glasses and joined her. "And now I know you can cook." Claire nudged him with her shoulder. "I'll be expecting a lot more of it."

"You bet," David grinned, making her middle pool with warmth. "I'd be happy for another excuse to spend time with you." He took a step closer, his arm brushing against hers.

Kissing him quickly on the cheek, Claire flipped on the faucet. "I'm holding you to that." She squirted soap on the sponge, feeling happiness. Happiness like she had experienced before Mom died. David slid right into the huge gaping hole in her heart, and she wondered how she ever existed without him. *Whoa, chill. You're leaving soon. Be careful.* Her mood instantly soured, vigorously she scrubbed the stuck-on cheese off a plate.

Under her breath she muttered, "Or at least until we have to move." Claire didn't look over at David, but instead focused on making sure each plate was squeaky clean before placing it into the dishwasher.

Silence. It made her skin crawl.

Shifting, David leaned against the kitchen counter facing her. He crossed his ankles and folded his arms. Claire didn't glance over at him, but kept her eyes trained on the Pyrex pan she was tackling to clean. Feeling his gaze on her, Claire's cheeks burned. Certainly, David could have any woman he wanted. Why was he wasting his time on her? Her life was nothing but a web of grief and baggage. She was leaving Pismo, and he needed to stay. The roadblocks weren't going away no matter how much she wanted them to.

Finally, after what felt like an eternity, David cleared his throat. "Can I help you load the dishwasher?" He ran a finger down the length of her arm, searching for her gaze. "Or would you prefer for me to dry the pots and pans?"

Claire didn't look over at him but handed him a dripping cup to put in the dishwasher.

His hands lingered over hers. "Everything okay?" Slowly, David put the glass onto the top rack of the dishwasher. "You are being awful quiet, plus you won't look at me."

Sucking in air, Claire paused in place, gripping the sink with both hands. "No, everything isn't okay." Her voice cracked, revealing everything trapped inside of her. Losing Mom, being forced to take an unwilling Alexis back to Los Angeles, meeting David at the worst possible time, but falling for him anyways, everything spun rapidly around in her head. "I'm leaving in like six weeks. What are we even doing together? I mean I'm playing with fire." She slammed a plate into the dishwasher without bothering to hand it to David.

"Claire..." David's was voice soft. He reached over and flipped off the faucet. Claire leaned against the sink, touching her shoulder to David's. Wrapping his arm around her shoulders, David continued, "Let's talk about this."

"Why did you have to be so wonderful?" Claire shrieked. Then she pinched the bridge of her nose. "You waltzed in here being Mr. Perfect. You are so easy to love. I mean you cooked dinner with my sister for crying out loud. And then right when things start to get good, we'll have to leave. Then what?"

David squeezed her shoulders. Shifting, Claire wrapped her arms around his middle. Melting against his chest, she listened to the steady beat of his heart. David's hand roamed down her hair and back in a rhythmic motion, making the nerves in her gut loosen.

"I thought," David said into her hair, "we decided we're going to enjoy spending time together while you're still here." His breath tickled her neck, sending goosebumps down her back. "Let's not worry about any of the things we can't control right now."

This didn't solve their issue. These weren't the words Claire wanted to hear.

With a quivering voice, Claire whispered, "I don't know if that's enough for me."

Deep down she knew the ticking clock of her departure wasn't going away. If anything, she wanted David to come up with some resolution on the spot. A miraculous way for them to remain together. So, what if she was thinking twelve steps too far ahead. Deep down, Claire knew this thing with David was different—special.

David's chest heaved under her cheek. "It isn't enough for me either." He shrugged. "But right now, it's all we have."

For a moment, Claire squeezed her eyes closed, focusing on the feeling of being in his arms without the worry of what tomorrow held. His spicy cologne tickled her nostrils while his strong arms held her steady. When she needed to leave Pismo, it would hurt, no question. It might gut her completely, leaving her heartbroken and alone. Even with the guarantee of heartache, today, Claire wasn't ready to say goodbye. Today, she wanted David. Six weeks left. She wished it was more, so much more, but some of David was better than none at all.

"Fine," Claire exhaled. "I'll worry about leaving and what that means for us when the time comes." She pulled away enough to glance up at him, searching his face for reassurance he felt the same. "I still want today with you."

Reaching out, David cupped her face between both of his hands. Her body buzzed, making her feel young and alive.

"I do too. We'll figure it out," whispered David. He leaned in, nearly making his lips graze hers. "Together."

Claire gulped, knowing full well a few weeks wouldn't be enough with David. Heck, five years wouldn't be, either.

"Together," repeated Claire.

Her gaze flickered between his eyes and his lips. Standing on her tiptoes, Claire crossed the few inches holding them apart, allowing her lips to glide across his. David tugged her closer, bringing them hip to hip. Her hand dove into his hair, raking it between her fingertips. His thumb danced across her chin.

In the kitchen, kissing David, Claire forgot about her heartache, pain, and grief. Here, with him, Claire believed she'd be okay, and whatever tomorrow held, she could bear it. He brushed his tongue along her bottom lip, making her lips tingle. His cologne, perfectly intoxicating, filled her lungs, making her knees wobbly.

Without missing a beat, David supported her weight, tightening his hold around her waist. Mind blank, Claire only dwelled on the sensation of his skin against hers. They kept kissing like tomorrow was tomorrow. And today was all that mattered.

How long they remained in the kitchen kissing, Claire didn't have a clue.

But the sudden, abrupt voice of Alexis broke the trance. "You've got to be kidding me," scoffed Alexis. "You two…" She shook her head and folded her arms, leaning against the doorframe leading into the kitchen.

Claire scurried out of David's arms, smoothing out her ruffled hair with her hand. She tugged her shirt back to its proper length, trying to appear cool, calm, and collected though her heartrate begged to differ.

Alexis continued, "I can't leave you two alone for a minute," she tsked, pivoting. "I need you to sign my progress report, when you're done making out," said Alexis over her shoulder. She continued down the hallway until completely out of sight.

"She does have a point." David reached out, tugging her back into his arms. "I can't help it if I love kissing you." He gave her a peck on the tip of her nose. "And I can't keep my hands off of you."

Claire fanned her face with her hand. Her cheeks burned, fiery and hot, but it didn't compare to the molten lava building inside of her. "I'm so embarrassed."

"Ahh…" David shrugged. "Don't be. I'm not. I don't care who sees us kiss."

Claire caught the hint of mischievousness in David's gaze.

"Really?" She put a hand on her hip. "You're telling me," pressing a finger into his rock-hard chest, "if it was your family, your parents, who caught us kissing you wouldn't be the least bit embarrassed?" She raised an eyebrow.

David rubbed the stubble on his jaw. "Okay, maybe." His gaze flickered across her face. He lowered his voice, "But for the record, I'd be thrilled for the entire world to know we were together."

Claire didn't know what to say in return, so, she simply leaned in and kissed him again.

CHAPTER TWELVE

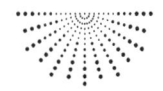

Unfortunately, the lights of the auditorium were lowered. In the darkness, David squinted, hoping for his eyes to adjust quickly to the dim lighting. A horrible accident on the freeway had resulted in him arriving ten minutes late to Alexis's dance recital in the neighboring town of San Luis Obispo. Due to a last-minute work emergency, David didn't drive over with Claire and Alexis as was previously planned.

According to Alexis, this wasn't a recital *per se*, but more of a performance involving a few different dance companies. Alexis invited him via text after cooking together. David had never attended a dance performance before and was excited to see Alexis in action. Any extra time with Claire was a bonus.

Unable to spot Claire, or an empty seat, David shot her a text hoping she could tell him the general location of where she was sitting. A packed auditorium, big enough for a few thousand, wasn't what he envisioned. This was a production. A huge fancy backdrop with decorations filled the stage. The ballerinas were dressed in fancy and ornate costumes.

David wondered if he should've dressed nicer than his

slacks and button-down shirt. He regretted not grabbing his sports coat on the way out of his house. Furthermore, he wished he wasn't forced to arrive so late. His phone vibrated in his pocket. Discreetly, David cupped his hand over the screen to cut back on the light while he read the message.

> Third row next to the right aisle.

David was on the wrong side of the auditorium. Exiting, he walked to the other side and reentered. Ducking down, he made his way to the correct row. Spotting Claire in her seat, David slipped into the row. Claire smiled and removed her jacket which she had placed on the seat next to her.

Sitting down, David leaned in and whispered, "I'm sorry I'm late. Did Alexis already go on?" He glanced at the stage, trying to see if he spotted Alexis.

"No. You made it in time," Claire whispered back with her gaze still glued to the stage. "She's in the next three numbers."

Claire found his hand, interlocking her fingers with his. Soon the number ended, and he clapped along with the rest of the audience. The music changed from a jazzy upbeat melody to the soothing sounds of a famous classical song he couldn't name, but recognized. Alexis *en pointe*, glided from off stage left toward the center with several other ballerinas. In perfect unison, the ballerinas went up *en pointe* then down again, followed by fast spins. Crisply, they turned together in tight circles. Around and around for what seemed like forever. David wondered how the dancers didn't get sick or dizzy. It was mesmerizing.

Then Alexis emerged, taking center stage with her dance partner. He lifted and spun her with a single hand high above his head. David marveled at Alexis's grace. With a twist, Alexis landed perfectly into her partner's arms. Immediately, the lights went dark, ending the number. The audience erupted in applause. David sprung to his feet, clapping louder than anyone else.

After the applause ended, the stage lit up again for the next number. David settled back into his seat, leaning toward Claire over the armrest, he whispered, "I didn't know Alexis was this good."

"I know," Claire smiled back. "She's talented. Maybe moving her to Los Angeles will give her bigger opportunities for dance." She shifted back, returning her attention back to the stage.

His stomach dropped like he was on weird elevator ride, knocking the wind right out him. Claire was leaving. Alexis was leaving too. And he'd be alone. Again. David knew it was happening, but naïvely he believed if he lived in the moment he wouldn't ever have to face the reality of their future. Wrong. Everyone always left him, first his ex-wife, and now Claire and Alexis. For the rest of the dance performance, David sat in a nauseated haze.

Finally, the last number ended, and the lights in the auditorium turned back on. People stood at once, moving down the rows toward the exit. With the shuffling, David mindlessly followed the crowd out in a daze. He made the mistake of not glancing back for Claire, and by the time he made it out of the auditorium and into the lobby he had lost sight of her. Running a shaky hand through his hair then down the length of his face, David questioned everything. His stomach twisted in a knot, making his hands clammy. Why had he allowed himself to fall for Claire when she was leaving—forever?

Scanning the crowd as people continued to spill out from the auditorium, David still didn't spot Claire. He moved out of the way of the traffic, leaning up against the wall. Pulling out his phone, he shot Claire a text.

> I lost you in the crowd. I'm waiting in the far side of the lobby for you.

He waited, pulling up a social media app to occupy himself. His phone dinged. He tapped on the message to open it.

> I know. You took off. I didn't even get a chance to talk to you. I'm waiting for Alexis to come out. If you're in a hurry to leave, you can go ahead and go.

The words stared back at him, making his insides churn. His behavior hadn't gone unnoticed. David hated how he had acted in haste. His fingers slid across the screen.

> Sorry. I've a lot on my mind. But I'll wait.

The three dots danced at the bottom of text chain, showing Claire was reading his message and typing up a response.

> It's fine. Just go. It might be a while.

David sucked in the air. His back went rigid.

> I want to wait with you. Where are you?

> Back inside the auditorium to the left. You'll see me with the other parents who are waiting.

> I'm coming.

> Ok

He slid his phone back into his pocket, pushing himself off the wall, David walked toward the back entrance of the auditorium. A few feet from the door, someone called his name. He turned toward the sound. Then unfortunately, his gaze landed on his ex-wife, Lauren, wrapped up in the arms of her new husband.

Jaw slack, David froze.

Lauren moved toward him, hand in hand with the guy who had taken David's place. "I thought that was you." Breathless, Lauren landed right in front of him. David had nowhere to escape. "What are you doing here?" She adjusted her purse strap, dropping her husband's hand.

Zach, her new husband, wrapped a protective arm around her.

The sight of them together made David's knees lock and hands form tight fists. "I should ask you the same thing," replied David, forcing himself to breathe.

"Zach's daughter was in the performance." Lauren glanced over his shoulder and around the lobby. "Why are you here? Are you here with someone?"

David folded his arms protectively against himself. "I'm here with a date." He fiddled with his watch, appearing to glance down at it, though he didn't even register the time. "I need to get going. She's waiting with the other parents for the dancers to come out."

"She's a parent too?" Lauren's gaze searched his face for more information. David tried his best to maintain a neutral expression, avoiding giving Lauren even an ounce of anything. "Well..." Lauren huffed. "We're headed there ourselves."

David paused. Zach remained quiet, averting his gaze to anywhere but on him. Maybe Zach finally found his conscience, seeing that Lauren and Zach's affair had broken up both of their marriages. But that might have been wishful thinking. Lauren on the other hand, seemed to hold zero guilt, pushing up her chin and squaring the shoulders of her skintight black dress.

Pressing for further information, Lauren asked in a voice meant to be innocent, "Does your date have a daughter too?"

His blood ran cold. David took the few remaining steps to the auditorium door. "Don't do that," said David over his shoulder.

Aggressively, David opened the door, nearly breaking his balance.

"Do what?" asked Lauren with a sickly-sweet voice.

Jaw tight, he replied, "Act like you care."

David entered the auditorium, refusing to glance back to see if Lauren and Zach were following him. But he didn't need to look, David could feel Lauren's presence only a few steps back. Weaving through the long rows of seats, David hoped to lose Lauren and Zach. The last thing he needed was for Claire to meet Lauren. Sure, his divorce would always be a part of his past, but he managed to avoid running into Lauren for three years. If he was lucky, he'd make it the rest of his life without seeing her again.

Though, knowing Lauren, David knew she'd make sure she wasn't ignored tonight. Lauren demanded to be seen at any cost. One quick glance back behind him, confirmed his worst nightmare, Zach and Lauren were on his tail. Spotting Claire on the other side of the auditorium, David swam through the sea of parents.

"Sorry," David managed once he landed next to Claire. Running a hand through his hair, David continued, "I didn't mean to bolt."

"I'm glad you didn't leave." Reaching out, Claire gave David's hand a slight squeeze. Her gaze roamed his face. "Alexis was excited you were coming, and she'd be disappointed you left without telling her congratulations."

Tugging at his collar, David asked, "What about you? Did *you* want to see me too?"

David knew he was acting foolishly, digging for confirmation when Claire never wavered in her interest for him. But seeing Lauren again, the woman who had rejected him and tossed him aside when she found someone new, was doing all sorts of things to his ego. Even though so much time passed, and David should be over it, seeing Lauren in the flesh made his wounds fresh, practically bleeding.

"Of course," said Claire. Tilting her head to the side, worry lines sprawled across her forehead. "Why wouldn't I want to see you?"

Rubbing the back of his neck, David shifted his weight. "I don't know." He stared blankly out at the crowd of parents surrounding them.

Raising an eyebrow, Claire asked, "Am I missing something?"

Then David didn't need to look, his heightened sense of awareness alerted him to Lauren's presence. His shoulders tightened, making his back straighten. Lauren's nearness made him uncomfortable in his own skin. Suddenly, he was small, inadequate, and he hated himself all over again.

"There you are," said a breathless Lauren. Tugging Zach forward by the sleeve of his sports coat, Lauren inched her way closer to Claire and David. Annoyingly, Lauren flipped her long blonde hair over her shoulder, making David's gut clench tight. If Lauren noticed the narrowing of his eyes and locked jaw, she didn't show it. Clearing her throat, Lauren pushed up her chin and continued, "I wanted to meet your date."

"Why?" David hissed. His tone was harsh, making him immediately regret it.

He hated showing Lauren how unhinged she still made him feel. He should be over her, and he was, but seeing the one who outright rejected you, does something to you. Things you never thought possible. Every bit of your self-work you've done goes out the window, and you find yourself right back to where you were the day they left.

Claire's eyes darted between David and Lauren then Zach. Looping her hands around the crook of David's elbow, her touch grounded him a tad. Silence followed, so wide and vast, he didn't know silence could be deafening.

Finally, Claire replied, "I'm Claire. Who are you?" She smiled back at Lauren and Zach.

"I'm Lauren." Lauren wrapped her arm around Zach's waist. "David's ex-wife." She squeezed Zach's middle, looking up at him with eyes that made David want to hurl. "And this is Zach, my husband." Reverting her glance back to Claire, Lauren narrowed her eyes.

"I see," slowly Claire nodded. Her lips formed a tight line. "It's nice to meet you."

Another awkward pause, then Claire being the brilliant, fantastic woman she was, managed to exchange some pleasantries with Lauren, while David stood frozen, unable to form a single coherent thought. He wanted to run, but he couldn't, so the rest of the conversation continued in a blur. David blacked out, managing only a few mumbled phrases, a nod here, but he couldn't focus or remember anything other than he hoped for Alexis to appear to end this whole miserable exchange.

Finally, to his great relief, Alexis along with the other dancers emerged from the side of the stage. Soon parents moved *en masse*, each hoping to reunite with their child. The chaos brought an abrupt halt to a conversation he didn't want to remember.

Up on her tiptoes, Claire waved to Alexis. "My sister's here." Tugging David away from Lauren and Zach, Claire declared, "We need to go." Claire pushed them forward through the throng of people, over her shoulder she said with a polite wave, "It was nice meeting you."

They blended into the sea of people, moving further and further away from Lauren and Zach until they slipped out of sight. David trailed along behind Claire, gripping onto her hand like she was a life raft.

Before they made it to Alexis, Claire tilted her head up to his. "Are you okay? You look pale, and you left me hanging, making me talk to your ex-wife and her husband without any help." She peered back toward Alexis nearly to them.

Hands clammy, David released his grasp from hers. Shoving them into his pockets, he couldn't rid himself of the uncertainty rising in him. Lauren managed to do what she did their entire marriage, annihilate his self-worth.

David cleared his dry, scratchy throat. "I'm sorry. I froze. Seeing Lauren after three years threw me for a loop." His body stiffened as he replayed the exchange over in his mind. "I really don't know…"

Claire put a hand on his forearm, settling the spiral of thoughts whirling around in his mind. "We'll talk about this later. I don't want Alexis involved in this." She turned toward Alexis, smiling brightly as her little sister arrived.

David's cheeks burned. A trickle of sweat ran down his back. Though it was stuffy and crowded, he knew his cold sweat wasn't due to his surroundings. No, it had everything to do with having to further explain the complexities of his failed marriage.

David plastered a smile on his face. "Alexis, you were amazing!" He held his arm out and gave her a quick side hug.

Beaming, Alexis asked, "Did you really think so?" She wrung her hands together, casting her glance down at her feet. "I messed up on one turn."

"Are you sure? You fooled me. I thought you were fantastic," said David with enthusiasm. "Claire told me you were talented, but I had no idea." He made a mind blown gesture.

Alexis stood up straighter. "I'm glad you think so." Her cheeks grew redder by the minute. "And I'm glad nobody could tell I messed up."

Claire shifted, looping her hands around the crook of Alexis's elbow. "You were stunning." She winked at David, loosening the knot wound up in his gut. "I, too, was amazed at how much you've improved since the last time I saw you."

"When was that?" questioned Alexis. "I don't remember."

They moved toward the exit of the auditorium, the crowd thinning around them with each step.

"Christmas. The Nutcracker." Claire's voice cracked. She bit her bottom lip. "Mom was so proud you landed the lead, she'd be proud of you today, too."

With misty eyes, Alexis said in an almost whisper, "I know." Dragging her feet, Alexis slowed her pace as they exited the auditorium and spilled into the lobby. "It wasn't the same with her not here."

Claire blinked rapidly. "I agree..." She swiped at the corners of her eyes. Holding her arms out for an embrace, Alexis entered them. Claire squeezed Alexis tightly. "But I'm glad I was here to see you."

Alexis nodded. David's heart clenched. He wondered how many times the sisters would be met with grief at their major life moments.

Breaking their embrace, Claire let out a long raspy breath. "I guess we'd better go." Her gaze skidded to David.

David nodded, holding open the lobby door for them to exit. Once outside, the sticky, salt air filled his lungs. Cool relief hit his skin. David needed to lighten the mood, anything to help the sisters not end the evening on a bad note.

"Can I buy you both some frozen yogurt to celebrate?"

David pulled his keys out of his pocket. "Or, do ballerinas not eat frozen yogurt?"

Pointing at her chest, Alexis said, "This ballerina does. Can we go back to Pismo Beach and go to Pismo Yogurt? I like that place the best. They have the best toppings."

"Sounds good to me." David looked to Claire for confirmation. "Does that work?" He raised an eyebrow.

Smiling again, Claire replied, "I'm not one to turn down an opportunity to be treated to frozen yogurt."

David wrapped his arm around Claire's waist, hoping to push away the interaction with Lauren from ruining their evening. She mirrored his movement, putting her arm around his middle. Maybe they'd be okay? Maybe they'd figure it out and find a way to be together? But a pit formed in his stomach, because deep down he knew this might be the beginning of the end.

CHAPTER THIRTEEN

"Do you think David was acting weird?" Claire scanned the crowded parking lot, hoping to find a free spot in the pier parking lot.

Being Friday night, the out of towners were, well, in town making the population of Pismo explode at the seams. Come Monday, Pismo would be half the size. Summertime always brought the crowds too, every day of the week. Then Claire remembered that by summer, she and Alexis would be in Los Angeles. The thought depressed her. Being in Pismo these past months made Claire question everything.

She gripped the steering wheel harder, making her knuckles turn white. Living with no thought of tomorrow wasn't exactly working. Her stomach twisted on itself. Something was off with David. She could sense it in her bones. No doubt seeing Lauren was a big part of it. He never talked about her, and only mentioned once he was divorced.

"No," Alexis's fingers froze on her cell phone screen. She shifted, glancing over at her. "Is something off between you two?"

Claire spotted someone walking to their car. Bringing the

car to a crawl, she followed them back to their car to take their spot. "David's ex-wife was at the dance performance."

Alexis's jaw dropped. Her eyes dilated. "Say what?"

Skillfully, Claire pulled into the tight spot and turned off the ignition. Flipping down the visor mirror, Claire scrutinized her appearance, wondering what Lauren thought of her, which was ridiculous, because who cared what a woman she met once thought of her? Grabbing her lipstick out of her purse, Claire reapplied her lipstick then closed the mirror and pushed the visor back up.

Tossing her lipstick inside her purse, Claire zipped it closed. She shifted in her seat to face Alexis. "Lauren, that's David's ex-wife, was there with her new husband. I don't know the whole story, but David acted like a deer in the headlights. He just froze, and I was forced to carry on a conversation with two people I don't even know."

Also, Claire didn't reveal he ditched her after the performance was over. Literally, he left without even looking over his shoulder. Maybe David spotted his ex-wife and was trying to avoid speaking to her? That would make sense.

Alexis unbuckled her seat belt. "Yikes. Ex-wife, awkward." She raised an eyebrow.

"You're telling me," Claire muttered under her breath.

"Do you think he's still in love with his ex-wife?" asked Alexis.

"No," Claire replied much too quickly. "I mean, I don't think it's like that, but then again, I don't know their history. But I do think seeing Lauren might have messed with David's head. Like maybe he isn't ready for anything with me."

"Perhaps…" Alexis opened her car door. "But I'm sure it's fine. You said the ex-wife was with her new husband. So, you've got nothing to worry about."

Pushing her door open too, Claire slipped out and shut her door. Alexis came around the car, stopping beside her.

Claire continued, "I'm not threatened by Lauren. I'm only worried about how seeing her might make David question if he's ready to move on, to be with me." She tried to shrug casually. "Maybe I'm only the rebound girl."

Alexis wrapped an arm around her shoulder. "Ahh, don't worry, big sis. David looks at you like you're the best thing since sliced bread. I don't think you're the rebound. I think David thinks you're the *one*. Why else would he spend time with you and fall further in love with you when we're moving?"

David's arrival from behind them made Claire jump. "Whoa, I didn't see you there," said Claire. Her hand flew to her chest.

"I'm sorry. I didn't mean to startle you. Are you ladies ready?" David shoved his hands into his pockets instead of reaching for Claire's hand.

He never did that before, but maybe Claire was imagining things.

Smoothing out her hair, Claire replied, "Yes. Let's go."

"Woohoo!" declared Alexis.

Alexis dashed toward the yogurt shop, leaving them a few feet behind. They walked the block from the pier parking lot to Pismo Yogurt in silence. A couple of times, Claire glanced over at David, but he stared straight ahead at the sidewalk. Right when Claire was going to ask if everything was okay, David reached for her hand, interlocking his fingers with hers. Claire melted against his arm, wanting to feel him close and settle the pounding in her temples. *We're okay. See? Nothing has changed. There's nothing to worry about.* Lies, all lies. She didn't need to see the distance to know that it was there.

Arriving at Pismo Yogurt, the small shop was vacant,

because only a half hour remained until they closed. Alexis didn't waste any time loading up her cup with vanilla yogurt and a mountain of candy toppings.

Claire picked the original tart and put some fruit on it. David selected chocolate with Oreos and peanut butter cups. After David paid, they sat at the table near the window facing the sidewalk which led to the pier. Even though the hour was late, people were still walking by in a steady stream. Their conversation stayed on Alexis's performance.

"I still can't get over that last lift," said David with spoon in hand. "I mean you nailed the landing. I'm so impressed." He took a bite of his yogurt.

Alexis paused, rubbing her hands back and forth over the sweatpants she had thrown over her leotard. "Was it when I went from my partner spinning me into the landing?"

David's face lit up. "Yep." He snapped then pointed. "That's the one. It was spectacular."

"It took me three weeks to master the spin and twist." Alexis smirked. "I knew you'd like ballet." She did a funky dance with her shoulders, while she took another bite of her yogurt.

Smiling, David replied, "I like watching *you* do ballet. Thanks for inviting me."

"You bet," said Alexis. "I'm glad you came."

"I liked the second to last number." said Claire as she took her last bite of yogurt. "The one where the ballerinas did triple spins in unison."

"Ahh, yes, we've been working on that for months." Done with her yogurt, Alexis tossed the empty cup and spoon into the neighboring trash can. Crossing her arms, she sighed, "I'm going to miss my dancer friends when we move." Her face slackened and shoulders drooped.

Alexis stared out the window. The air became static, sucking the playful retelling of the night away. Silence hovered around their table. Claire didn't look over at David but felt his gaze on her. It made her skin itchy.

Claire wrung her hands together. "I'm sure you'll miss Pismo. I will too. But we'll make sure we come to visit." She managed a forced smile. Her heart ached to think of what she was leaving, especially David.

"It won't be the same." Shaking her head, Alexis stared out the window. "Nothing will ever be the same."

Claire caught Alexis's glance in the reflection of the window. "No, it won't," said Claire softly. "But we'll be okay."

An employee stopped in front of their table. "We're closing up," said the employee.

David stood. "No problem. We'll head out. Thanks." He pushed in his chair and gathered up his trash.

Standing too, Claire tossed her trash. "Sorry, we didn't realize the time."

David strode to the door, holding it open for Claire and Alexis to exit. As they walked toward the parking lot, a voice called out Alexis's name.

Glancing up the street, Claire squinted her eyes as they adjusted to the darkness of night. Juliet ran toward them.

"Alexis!" Juliet arrived in front of them out of breath. "I thought that was you. Are you leaving? Or do you have time to hang out? I'm headed to the arcade with my mom and brother. Do you want to come?"

Waving at Juliet's mom and brother, Claire smiled then glanced at Alexis.

Shifting toward Claire, Alexis clasped her hands together and pleaded, "Please, can I go?"

Claire glanced at her watch. "Sure," she held up a finger. "But only for a half hour."

Alexis and Juliet ran off together, catching up to where Juliet's mom and brother were waiting. Once they were out of sight, Claire inched toward David. "Do you want to go for a walk so we can talk?"

David ran a hand down the length of his face. "We can go for a walk." His shoulders dropped. "But it doesn't mean I'm excited about what you want to talk about."

"I'm sure that's true." Claire shifted her weight, glancing down the sidewalk toward the ocean and pier. "Do you want to walk the pier or the sand?"

"Sand," replied David.

Claire nodded, shoving her hands into her pockets. The ocean breeze nipped at her skin, making her shiver. They walked in silence the remaining block to the beach. Waves crashed on the shore, making the sound vibrate through her. Once at the edge of the sand, both stopped and removed their shoes, carrying them with them.

David reached for her hand with his free hand, leading her closer to the water's edge where the sand was firm and smooth and easier to walk on. Their footprints left a trail behind them. Only the lights from the pier along with the stars up in the sky lit their way. Claire wondered who would speak first.

Finally, David broke the quiet. "Lauren left me," stated David. His voice cracked. "We met in college. I was crazy about her, and I couldn't wait to marry her. As soon as we graduated, we got married..." His voice drifted off, stopping, he stared out at the ocean.

Claire came to a halt beside him, giving his hand a reassuring squeeze and not wanting to interrupt, she waited for him to continue.

David let go of her hand and rubbed the back of his neck. Glancing over at her, he asked, "Do you mind if we sit for a while?"

And Claire saw it, written in his eyes. This was their end, and Claire didn't know how to stop it.

Maybe it was the chilly air, but Claire's teeth started to chatter. "Sure." She tried to sound casual, but her heart thundered.

They walked up the small sandy hill to where the sand was dry. Dropping her shoes, Claire plopped herself down on the sand. David sat down next to her, cradling his knees with his arms.

Both stared out at the seemingly endless view of ocean. Claire's hands shook, and she placed them underneath her, sitting on top of them. The pounding of her heart made her anxious. When David didn't continue, Claire said, "So, what happened next?"

David's chest heaved with a long exhale. "What *didn't* happen?" He shook his head, glancing down at his feet. "We married. I thought we were happy and in love, but I still had dental school then an orthodontics residency. It was long and hard, and I probably wasn't the best spouse to Lauren. She was alone a lot. I wished she hadn't been, and I regret that part. Lauren proved to be overly critical of me. Anything I did was wrong. I never made her happy. I knew we weren't doing great, but I thought things would get better. If I could just finish school and start my own practice, then we could be happy. Then we'd have money, and I'd have more time.

"But one day out of the blue I came home, and Lauren told me she was moving out. I was completely blindsided. She told me she met someone new. Zach. They'd been carrying on together for a while behind my back." David shifted, leaning back on both of his hands at his sides. He stretched his legs out and crossed his ankles. "I was too late to fix anything, and she didn't even want to try. She loved Zach and not me and that was that."

Claire tilted her head toward him, taking in the entire image of him. She wondered how anyone could ever stop loving David. He was the most loveable guy she'd ever met.

Kind and thoughtful, patient and understanding, and it broke her heart Lauren hadn't seen what only took her one day to see. David was someone worth rewriting your entire life for, not someone you left.

Drawing a circle in the sand with her finger, Claire replied, "I'm sorry. I can't imagine. It must've been heartbreaking. For you to have everything you ever wanted and then have it disappear. I'm sorry your marriage didn't work out."

"It was horrible because I loved Lauren. I wanted to be with her, but Lauren didn't love me anymore. I often wonder whether she ever really loved me." David straightened his back, running his hand through his hair. "It still hard. I struggle. I question my worth. I think I'm unlovable. Sometimes I question if I have what it takes to ever get married again. It terrifies me to give my heart over to someone and know I could have it happen again—divorce. I couldn't do it. It would break me."

"I can't argue with you. I think those are valid concerns." Claire rubbed her hands together to rid them of the sand. Desperately, she wanted to wrap her arm around David and tell him, she chose him. He was special and Lauren was a fool, but David already seemed so distant. Like she'd already lost him, and there wasn't a way to get him back. Clearing her throat, she said, "But maybe the second time around you'll get it right. You'll find the right person. Maybe you'll be happier than you ever imagined, and Lauren will become a distant memory, and your doubts will disappear."

David shrugged. "Maybe," he mumbled.

"So, seeing Lauren again, did it…" Claire stumbled over her words, unsure of how to say the things bottled up inside of her. She mustered up the courage to continue, "make you question us?"

David shifted, wrapping his arm around Claire's

shoulders. She leaned into the warmth radiating off his body. "I don't know. I don't know about anything anymore. Seeing Lauren has messed with my head. I wished it hadn't, but it did."

Claire's insides churned on themselves. David might still love Lauren, and he might never stop loving her. And Claire was leaving in a month. It was a double sucker punch to the gut.

Cradling her knees, Claire said, "So what are you saying? Do you think you're not ready to be with me?"

"I'm beginning to see I got swept up in the idea of you," said David. "I really enjoy being around you and Alexis, but I don't know. I just don't know..." His voice trailed off, and he stared down at his feet.

His words stung. Wiggling out of his arms, Claire grabbed her shoes beside her. "I'm leaving in a month." Claire stood and brushed the sand off her backs
ide with her free hand. "Maybe we shouldn't pretend anymore that it isn't happening."

"I..." David stumbled to his feet, swiping his sandy hands on his pants. He bent back down and picked up his shoes. "I know you're leaving, but I enjoy spending time with you and Alexis. I want to hang out with you until you both move."

Hang out? Is that what they've been doing? She was so blind, and she hated herself for believing David was falling for her too. In her pain and sorrow, her judgement was impaired. Impaired enough to have her make choices she never should've made.

Claire moved first, walking back toward the pier. "I think this should be the last night we see each other." She didn't wait for him.

David jogged to catch up with her. "Why? I don't understand. We said we'd wait until you moved to worry about the future."

Claire didn't slow down, taking fast strides to get back to the sidewalk. He didn't get it. Not at all. Claire *loved* him. David only saw her as a distraction. A project to fill his time. When they reached the edge of the sand, Claire stopped to put back on her shoes.

"What did I say?" David bent down and put on his shoes too. "Claire, talk to me."

The fact David didn't even know, told Claire everything she didn't want to believe.

Glancing up the sidewalk, Claire spotted Alexis with Juliet a few blocks away. She waved, and Alexis waved back. "David…" Her voice cracked. She hated how much she cared, how much her heart was ripping out of her chest. "I appreciate everything you've done to help me and Alexis, but we're fine." She met his gaze. "We leave in a month, and I don't see the point in dragging this out. I wish you nothing but the best."

"But," David reached to touch her arm.

Claire took a step forward out of reach of his grasp. "Bye David." She shoved her hands into her pockets and walked away, leaving him lingering on the sidewalk.

She thought he'd call out for her. But he didn't. She hoped he would jog to catch up with her, but he stayed in his place. So, Claire walked away, and David let her go.

CHAPTER FOURTEEN

THE WEEK PASSED IN A HAZE.

And the next.

And another.

Then another.

David had messed up, and he knew it. Claire had been right, she was leaving and there wasn't any point in dragging out the inevitable. But boy, he wished it didn't hurt so much.

David went to reception where Sarah was typing on the computer. "Sarah, do you know how many more appointments I have today?" He usually didn't feel this anxious for the workday to end, but his body was dragging.

Sarah stopped typing and moved her mouse, bringing up the schedule for the day. Swiveling in her chair to face him, she said, "It looks like only three more appointments for the day. I did squeeze Alexis in for one more adjustment before she heads out of town. It's a week earlier than normal, but I figured you wouldn't mind."

David froze. "Alexis is coming in today?" He hadn't been prepared to see Alexis, or Claire.

He missed Claire more than he ever thought possible. But like an idiot he did nothing.

"Yes." Sarah leaned back in her chair, folding her arms. "She's the last appointment of the day." She raised an eyebrow. "Everything okay? You usually don't care or worry about when people are coming in."

Grabbing a client's file off the corner of the reception desk, David flipped it open. "Everything is fine." His hands shook. He forced himself to turn to the next page and appear put together. Though he was far from it, instead he was slowly unraveling. Eyes glued to the file, he continued, "Let's make sure we find a time for them to return to do a follow up appointment. It might not be the exact timing of the normal adjustments but let's make it work for them."

Sitting up, Sarah replied, "You've got it boss."

The door chimed, entering the lobby was his next client. David smiled, pushing away the ball of nerves in his gut. "Hunter, it's great to see you. Today's the day," he said brightly.

Hunter beamed. "I can't wait to get my braces off and see what my teeth look like."

"I can't either. It's the best part of my job." David closed the file folder still in his hands, motioning for Hunter to follow him back to the exam room. "In thirty minutes, you're going to have a beautiful, straight teeth smile."

"Yippee!" replied Hunter.

After taking Hunter into the exam room, David's dental assistant helped Hunter get settled into his chair while he checked on the adjustments of two other waiting patients. The remaining hours flew by. Next thing he knew, David glanced over to see Alexis waiting in one of the many exam chairs.

His shoulders stiffened. Peering around the room, he didn't spot Claire. He wondered if she was in the waiting room or opted to avoid him all together. David walked over and sat down on the swivel chair next to Alexis.

Alexis glanced up at him from her reclined position and rolled her eyes. "You don't need to worry, Claire isn't here. She dropped me off and is grabbing us some dinner. If you want, you can completely avoid her when she comes back to pick me up."

"I don't need to avoid her," said David a little too quickly. "Claire is the one who ended things, not me." Each word punctured the air, sounding off-putting even to him. David grabbed Alexis's chart off the corner of the table next to the exam chair, opening it up. He fisted his shaky hand and tried his best to regain his exposure.

"Uh huh..." Alexis muttered under her breath. She turned back, settling her head against the head rest. "You keep telling yourself that."

David controlled his desire to argue and explain he wanted to spend the last month with them in Pismo, but he knew it was fruitless. He didn't have any way to rectify the situation, and now the month was over, and they were leaving for good.

Lowering the back of her chair to a flatter position, David replied, "Let's see how your teeth are looking."

Alexis complied, opening her mouth. With a gloved hand, David poked and prodded her mouth, trying to gauge how many more adjustments were needed to complete Alexis's treatment. He tightened the necessary braces, then removed and replaced the position of a few brackets.

After stripping off his gloves and making some notes on Alexis's chart, Alexis asked, "How many more visits do you think it will take before I get my braces off? Claire wanted me to ask."

Scribbling down the last notes, David shifted to the computer, pulling up x-rays of Alexis's teeth. He leaned forward double checking the current position of her two back molars. Finally, he peered at Alexis, "I think you will have to come two more times. You're close. You can get them off before summer ends. How does that sound?"

Alexis smiled for the first time, melting away the permanent scowl on her face since arriving. "I think it will work if Claire can get the time off. She starts back at her physical therapy job on Monday."

"If you need to come up on a weekend, I can come in on a Saturday to do the adjustments," replied David.

"Okay, I'll tell her." Alexis swung her legs over the side then stood. "See you later, Dr. Clark."

Her calling him Dr. Clark made his shoulders tense. "Alexis…"

Alexis twisted around, facing him. She raised an eyebrow, waiting.

His shoulders drooped. "Tell Claire I'm sorry, for everything."

"You tell her." Alexis moved to leave. "Don't make me do your dirty work." She left the exam room, walking through to the waiting room.

David knew Claire was in there, because he'd heard her greet Sarah at reception a few minutes ago. He grabbed Alexis's chart. With weak knees, David found his balance and forced himself to walk into the waiting room. He went to the reception desk without glancing around.

Sarah glanced up from her desk. "Dr. Clark, they're completely set. I scheduled Alexis's next appointment for four weeks from today."

Clearing his throat, David held out Alexis's chart to Sarah. "Thanks for scheduling her appointment. Here's her chart for you to enter the information into the computer." Sarah took the chart from him.

Finally, David shifted, gazing out at the waiting room. It

contained only Claire and Alexis. When David locked eyes with Claire, she shuffled her feet and adjusted her purse on her shoulder. Gripping the strap tightly with one hand, it made her knuckles turn white.

Pushing up her chin, Claire said, "Thanks. We'll see you in a month." She moved toward the door, waving for Alexis to follow. "Come on, Alexis. It's time to go."

"Bye, Dr. Clark," Alexis mumbled.

David couldn't find the words to explain the emotions bottled up in him, but he hated things being this strained between them. They exited, making the chime from the door ring in his ears.

Move. Now. David strode to the lobby door, swinging it open. Alexis and Claire were already halfway to their car.

"Wait!" David called out. In tandem, they both stopped. Rotating to face him, Claire and Alexis exchanged a quick look before staring blankly back at David. "Wait," he repeated, jogging toward them, "please."

Alexis folded her arms. David half expected her to make an excuse and go wait in the car, but she didn't move. Alexis stood her ground, gripping Claire's forearm.

Scratching his chin, before shoving both shaking hands into his pockets, David cleared his throat, "I'm sorry for how things ended."

Claire blinked. "Okay," she said dismissively, looking down at her red painted nails. "We're good."

"Okay?" David questioned.

"Okay. Dr. Clark." Claire half pivoted toward her car. Alexis mirrored her movements. "We'll see you in a month." Taking a step away from him, the gap widened between them. "Thank you for generously agreeing not to charge us the remaining balance."

So, Claire called him Dr. Clark too. Boy, he was in it deep. "Can I call you sometime?" David sputtered out.

David liked being around Claire. He'd missed having her in his life this past month.

Claire glanced over at Alexis. The two exchanged a look David couldn't quite figure out, but Alexis turned and walked the remaining few yards to the car and climbed in. Claire confirmed Alexis was out of ear shot.

Raising an eyebrow, Claire asked, "And why would you want to call me?"

"Because I like talking to you." David rubbed the back of his neck. He wished knew how to express himself better. Honestly, he didn't know if he'd ever be ready to move on, but things with Claire were the closest he ever came to opening his heart again after Lauren. "And I'm going to miss seeing you."

Shaking her head, Claire cast her gaze back toward Alexis in the car. "I don't think it's a good idea for you to call me."

"Why not?" David pressed.

Claire gnawed on her bottom lip. "Because I *liked* you." She wrung her hands together. "And I realize now it was one sided. I won't do that to myself again." She walked the rest of the way to her car. After opening her car door, she glanced over her shoulder and said, "We'll see you in a month. Bye, David."

Then she climbed in and drove away.

CHAPTER FIFTEEN

"Alexis, are you almost ready?" Claire stood by the door of her apartment in Los Angeles. "I can't be late on my first day back."

Running into the foyer, Alexis threw a few things into her gym bag, zipping it closed. "I'm ready." She swung the bag over her shoulder. "Let's go."

Claire waved her through the door, before turning to lock up. They walked down the hallway to the elevator. "Do you remember how to catch the bus back home after your dance classes?"

"Yes," Alexis groaned. Then she playfully slapped Claire on the arm. "Quit worrying. I'm going to be fine."

"Huh?" Claire paused, studying her. "Last night you told me I ruined your life by making you move here."

Alexis waved it off. "I know, but that was yesterday. Today I'm resolved. We're here. There's nothing I can do about it. I might as well make the most of it." Nonchalantly, she shrugged.

Claire stopped in front of the elevator, pushing the down button. "I'm impressed. It's all very mature of you."

"That's me," Alexis gave a false smile while watching the floor number slowly inch closer to their floor, "Ms. Mature."

"So, Ms. Mature, do you remember the bus number?" Claire's stomach twisted in knots. Los Angeles wasn't Pismo.

Claire wondered if Mom would let Alexis ride the bus from her dance studio to their apartment. But then she reminded herself, she didn't have any other choice. Work was imperative at this point because Claire needed to replenish her dangerously low bank account. With Alexis as her responsibility now, Claire needed to better plan for their financial future.

Alexis scoffed. "We've been over this a thousand times. I'll be fine."

The elevator doors swung open. Both entered.

Gnawing on a fingernail, Claire forced her hand away to hit the garage button. "You'll be fine." She repeated it out loud, mostly to reassure herself.

After dropping Alexis off at her new dance studio, Claire drove the few miles to the hospital where she worked. Slowly, she walked through the familiar sliding glass doors into the hospital lobby. So much time had passed since she last worked, Claire wondered if she even remembered how to do her job anymore. But then the tension between her shoulder blades lessened with each step. For the first time, she realized how much she had missed this place, her co-workers, and the patients.

Riding the elevator up to the physical therapy gym, Claire wondered how much had changed since her abrupt departure. As she stepped off the elevator and entered the reception area, balloons and a huge sign saying *welcome back* greeted her. Claire smiled. And she knew she would be okay. With time, her mind would forget about Pismo and David. Her life might even start to feel like her life again.

"Claire!" shrieked Jennifer, Claire's co-worker, and friend.

Jennifer came around the reception desk. "You're back!" Jennifer held her arms out.

"I'm back," Claire hugged her. They broke their embrace. "I'm sorry I didn't ever call you back." Suddenly Claire realized how much she had isolated herself over the past months, pushing away the people who once mattered to her. The darkness of losing Mom and taking care of Alexis left her little room for anything else. She fiddled with loosened wisps of her hair, then reached up and retightened her ponytail. "I was in complete survival mode."

Jennifer linked arms with hers, leading her to the break room to drop off her things. "I figured." She patted the top of Claire's arm. "I only wish I could've helped you in some way. I'm sorry for everything you've been through, but I'm glad you're back."

Her eyes stung, and Claire blinked rapidly to force the emotions away. "I know. I missed you too." Her throat constricted. A whirling monsoon of thoughts wreaked havoc in her mind. "And, Jennifer…"

"Yeah," replied Jennifer.

"If you don't mind…" Claire forced herself to swallow. "I don't want to talk about my time in Pismo. I don't have the emotional bandwidth to rehash everything that happened while I was there. I'm here now, and I'm more than ready to be distracted with work."

Glancing over at her, Jennifer gave a quick nod. "No problem. You bet."

They entered the break room. Claire found her old locker, placing her things inside it. Once done, she peered around the familiar space. "It's surreal to be back after so much time," stated Claire.

With a hand on her hip, Jennifer grabbed the clipboard off the wall. It listed the schedule of appointments for the day. "You said you're ready to be distracted by work." She flipped through the pages, finding Claire's name. Jennifer ran her finger across the paper until she located the line with Claire's appointments. Claire took a step closer to view the clipboard. "You won't have to worry about down time, because you have back-to-back to appointments the entire morning."

"Welcome back, I guess," Claire stated then she forced a smile. "Bring it on."

With a warm smile, Jennifer said, "You were born ready."

Claire couldn't help but laugh. Clapping her hands together, Claire replied, "I guess I was."

The day sped by. With each new appointment, Claire quickly found her rhythm again of coming up with a plan for each patient, leading them through the various strength training exercises, and giving them a list of things to do on their own. She had missed her work. And most importantly, it took her mind off her life. Plus, she didn't think about David once.

After finishing her shift, Claire sang along to the radio driving home, finding herself in a better mood than she'd felt in ages. She even picked up some take-out Chinese food on the way home, in hopes Alexis's first day was a good one too.

Unlocking the front door, Claire *almost* felt happy. "Alexis, I'm home," she declared.

Claire removed her shoes by the door, dumping her purse and other things next to them. Wandering through the apartment back to the kitchen with food in hand, Claire called out for Alexis again. When she didn't emerge immediately, her stomach clenched tight. She wondered if Alexis hadn't made it home okay. Placing the food on her two-top dining table, Claire went in search of her sister. The door to her spare bedroom, now Alexis's room, was closed.

Knocking lightly on the door, Claire asked if she could enter. When she didn't hear a response, Claire opened it anyways.

Then lo and behold, Alexis was face planted on her twin bed fast asleep. Claire went over and shook her lightly. "Alexis," whispered Claire. Alexis wasn't an easy one to wake up. "Alexis. I'm home." Claire shook her shoulder a second time.

Groggily, Alexis slowly opened her eyes. "You're home." She flipped to her back, stretching her arms high above her head. Claire sat down on the corner of the bed. Alexis swung her legs over the side, sitting next to her. "I'm so tired. The new dance studio is no joke. It's twice as hard as the place in Pismo. I thought the instructor would never let us leave." She swiped at her eyes. Her blinking returned to normal.

"Other than that," Claire bit the inside of her cheek, "did it go okay? Were the other dancers nice? Did you get lost riding the bus?" Questions came in rapid succession, whirling around in her head.

"Whoa..." Alexis ran a hand over her head. Her hair was still in a tight bun. She started pulling out some of the bobby pins, loosening her hair. "I only just woke up. Give me a minute."

Nervously, Claire laughed. It was amazing how much she worried about Alexis. Quickly, without noticing, she had transitioned from sister to parent. "Okay, I'll try." Claire waited.

Once Alexis removed the bobby pins from her hair, she vigorously shook her head. Placing the bobby pins on her bed stand, Alexis exchanged them for her phone and slid it into the pocket of her jogger pants.

Alexis stood and said, "David texted me."

Claire froze. "He did?" She forced her expression to

remain impartial. She tried to not let on that his very name made her stomach do funky things. "And what did he want?"

With shaky knees Claire stood, wandering out of Alexis's room. Alexis followed her to the kitchen.

"Only to wish me luck on my first day at the new dance studio," replied Alexis.

Once in the kitchen, Claire unloaded the cartons of take-out food from the plastic to-go bag, placing them on the counter. "How did he know you were starting dance today?"

Alexis went to the cupboard, taking out two plates. "Because I told him."

With a carton in hand, Claire eyed Alexis suspiciously. "Since when have you been texting David, I thought you were mad at him, and on my side."

Swiveling back around, Alexis placed the plates on the counter and opened the Chinese noodles, spooning some onto her plate. "He texted me after we left his orthodontist's office."

"Oh, did he?" Claire tried her to act nonchalant, focusing on opening each carton. "And what did he say then?"

Reaching for the orange chicken, Alexis opened it and spooned some onto her plate next to her noodles. "David apologized for hurting me and asked if we could stay in touch." She shrugged. "I told him sure. But I won't text him again if you don't want me to."

Claire wondered why he hadn't bothered to contact her. Then she remembered David was doing exactly what she instructed him to do. "How about that," stated Claire.

Alexis stopped spooning food onto her plate. "You're not mad are you?"

"No," Claire whipped her hair over her shoulder. "David's a nice guy. He can ask about you. I'm glad he cares." Claire dished herself out some food from the various cartons and took her plate to the table and sat. Alexis joined her. Claire ignored her impulse desire to ask for more information, to pry every detail out of Alexis, hoping David had asked about her.

Digging into her fried rice, Claire continued, "So, Alexis, tell me about this super hard dance studio."

And the subject of David was dropped.

CHAPTER SIXTEEN

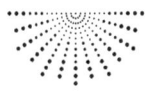

Adjusting her napkin on her lap, Kelly asked, "David, can you pass me the gravy?"

"Sure," David stopped eating and reached for the gravy, holding it out to Kelly. She took it from him and covered her meat with it. "Thanks again, Mom, for making my favorites." He took another bite of the carne asada.

Stephen grabbed another corn on the cob, placing it on his plate. "Yes, thanks honey." Next, he added some toppings to his baked potato. "It's delicious."

Kelly smiled, waving off their compliments. "My pleasure."

They ate for a few minutes in silence. Outside on the patio, the ocean waves competed against the squawking seagulls. David enjoyed the view, wishing for the serenity of the water to wash away his feelings of emptiness. It didn't. David missed Claire, and Alexis too.

Three weeks. They left three weeks ago, and time had moved so slowly David wondered if it was moving backwards. He couldn't even get lost in work, which was a first. Work always pushed out the noisy chaos in his life. Not this time. This was different. The void couldn't be filled with anything. And it was his fault. If he hadn't flipped when he saw Lauren, he might not have pushed Claire away. He might have found a way for them to be together, even if there was some physical distance at first.

Breathing in the tangy salt air, David hoped for the tightness in his chest to settle.

Suspiciously, Kelly eyed him up and down midbite. "What's up with you? You seem…" She waved a hand in his direction. "Off. No offense, but you look terrible."

"Thanks?" Shifting in his chair, David cut into his meat, ignoring Kelly. Pushing up his chin, he replied, "I'm perfectly fine." He shoved the meat into his mouth and reverted his gaze to the ocean.

A myriad of emotions ran through him, but he wasn't sharing them.

Silence. Only the pulsating beat of his heart sounded in his ears.

Breaking the pause in the conversation, Stephen asked, "Are you still hung up on seeing Lauren? Kelly told me how you saw her a few weeks back." He raised an eyebrow. "Please tell me you aren't dwelling on Lauren again, because I think you've punished yourself enough when it comes to her."

David scoffed. "No," he firmly said. "I'm not hung up on her." His jaw clenched tightly.

He wasn't hung up on Lauren, he was hung up on how she made him feel. Like he wasn't worth loving. Like he didn't deserve her, nor anyone for that matter.

Kelly shook her head, taking a bite of her baked potato. "David…" Her voice trailed off. She pulled her gaze from David to the ocean.

Stephen reached over, giving David's shoulder a squeeze. "David, when are you going to stop letting Lauren ruin your life? It's time, son. Time to move past her and allow yourself to be happy."

Aggressively, David wiped his face with his napkin then tossed it down with gusto. He shook off Stephen's hand. Pushing out his chair, David said, "I don't know, Dad. I guess I'll do that when it stops hurting so much." He stood, grabbing his half empty plate. "I'm getting the dessert out of the fridge." David turned to Kelly. "You made pie, right?"

Kelly nodded, gazing right through him to his broken heart. He hated how well Kelly knew him, and how without saying anything she knew exactly what he was thinking.

"Great," David pivoted and left, wandering into the kitchen.

Once inside the solitude of the kitchen, David placed his plate in the sink. Gripping the countertop with both hands, he forced himself to calm down by taking several deep breaths. He wished he didn't still feel this way. Like a rejected loser whose wife up and left him because she didn't love him anymore. Was he that pathetic? Was he such a horrible person to be around? His mind whizzed with the familiar catalog of his blaringly obvious faults. If Claire knew the real him, she'd know he did her a favor by cutting her loose.

Swinging open the fridge, David willed his dark thoughts of inadequacies away. After locating the pie, David took it and some more plates and a knife back out to the patio.

His parents had finished eating. They whispered to one another, but they stopped suddenly as he walked through the sliding glass door. David knew he was the topic of their private conversation. No doubt, they were worried he might never rebound from his divorce. Heck, even he wondered if it was possible.

David held up the pie and plates. "I've got the pie."

"I can see that." Kelly's lips formed a tight line. "Are we going to talk about what just happened?"

"Not a chance," David sat down, placing the pie and plates on the table.

"Fine, if that's how you want it." Kelly grabbed the pie, dragging it across the table so she could cut into it. "On another vein, and not to get you upset again, I wanted you to know I offered up our house for Claire and Alexis to stay at while they come down next weekend to get Alexis's braces adjusted."

Inhaling, David leaned back in his chair, cupping the back of his head with both of his hands. "How did you even know they were coming into town?" He raised an eyebrow.

Slapping the first piece of pie on a plate, Kelly held it out to Stephen. Stephen took the pie and placed it in front of himself. Kelly cut into the pie again.

"Sarah mentioned it when we saw her at the grocery store last week," said Kelly.

Shaking his head, David rubbed the back of his neck. "I should fire her for giving out that information."

Kelly held a plate with pie out to him. "You'll do no such thing." She gave him a challenging stare. David took the plate of pie from her, placing it in front of himself. Kelly continued, "Besides, I figured it was my Christian duty to offer a place for them to stay. I know money is tight for them. Isn't that why they moved back to Los Angeles?"

Cutting into his pie with his fork, David took a bite before he responded. If he remembered correctly, it was Kelly who cautioned him about becoming involved with Claire and Alexis. Kelly knew things had ended with Claire before she left Pismo.

"Yes," David cut another piece of the pie, eating his emotions. "They moved because they didn't have a choice, and money is tight for them, so I think it's kind of you to offer them your house as a place to stay. I'm sure they are appreciative."

Kelly served herself a piece of pie. "I spoke with Claire…" She licked off the bits of pie on her finger. "They're coming up on Friday for the appointment. Claire has some things to settle with the attorney too, and Alexis wants to hang out with her friends, so I told her to stay till Sunday and drive back in the afternoon."

Claire and Alexis here for an entire weekend. His lungs burned. Claire away in Los Angeles was one thing, but knowing she was here, in Pismo, was a whole other animal.

David shrugged, taking another bite of his pie. "Okay, thanks for letting me know."

Kelly hovered her fork over her pie. "I'm…" she paused, biting her bottom lip. "I'm okay with you dating her."

"What?" David's jaw dropped. He took a sip of his water. "Too bad, mom. That ship has sailed. Claire moved to Los Angeles. I live in Pismo." He glanced out at the ocean. "It is what it is."

Stephen wrapped his arm around Kelly. "Let's drop this whole thing. David's a big boy. He can decide who and when he wants to date someone."

Kelly exhaled, throwing up her hand. "I'll let it go, but I see I made a mistake in warning you against dating her. I didn't want to see you hurt when she left."

David was losing his patience. He gripped his hands into fists under the table. "Too late."

"I saw how happy you were when Alexis and Claire were in your life." Kelly glanced away, out at the ocean. For a long time, she didn't say anything, finally she continued, "And now you're not. I'm sorry I interfered. I wish I hadn't." She exhaled, making her shoulders droop.

When David didn't speak, Kelly slowly took a bite of her pie. Everything inside of him was a jumbled mess. And David had no idea how to unpack any of it, so he simply finished his pie.

CHAPTER SEVENTEEN

Rolling down the windows two inches, Claire allowed the tangy salt air from the ocean breeze to filter through the car. Driving down the two-lane highway hugging the Pacific Ocean, the tension between her shoulder blades loosened with each passing mile. Los Angeles drew further and further away, and Pismo came closer. Going home, her real home, if only for the weekend, made her smile.

Pulling Alexis out of school at lunch, they beat most of the Friday gridlock traffic from Los Angeles past Santa Barbara. With their current cruising rate, Alexis was going to be on time for her orthodontist appointment.

David.

She sighed.

Her lungs burned and skin itched at the thought of seeing him again. In her mind, she practiced her best neutral responses and vowed to not reveal how she was still hung up on him.

Glancing out her window, the rhythmic crashing of the waves pushed back at whatever was bubbling up. Her mind drifted to Mom. Claire turned down the radio, clearing her throat. "I think we should make time to go by Mom's grave tomorrow, they finally have the headstone on, and I want to see it before we leave."

Alexis stopped fiddling with her phone. Her fingers froze on the screen, peering over at her. "I agree, I think I'm ready to go by the gas station too," replied Alexis.

Gripping the steering wheel tighter, Claire's chest pinched tight. Her pulse thundered in her veins and with her free hand she swiped at her slick brow. Stealing a glance at Alexis, she asked, "Do you think you're really ready?"

Claire wasn't ready, but then again, she doubted she'd ever be.

"We can't avoid the place forever." Alexis stared out her passenger side window, rolling down the window completely to let her arm hang out the side. She widened her fingers, letting the air pass between them. "There are only a handful of gas stations," Alexis spoke loudly over the vibrating sound of the humming engine and fresh flowing air, "it's starting to get annoying to drive a mile out of the way to get gas." Her voice trailed off.

Claire found it hard to breathe. *Whoosh. Whoosh. Whoosh.* The air plowed through the car taking with it her last bit of self-preservation. Could she finally return to the place where Mom took her last breath? Was Claire strong enough to replace a horrible memory with good ones? Alexis was ready, Claire was the older sister after all, which meant she needed to follow her lead even if it proved to be painful.

Gritting her teeth, Claire forced herself to respond. "You might be right." She glanced once more out the window, then concentrated her attention on the upcoming curve in the road. One side of the car hugged chiseled mountain rock while the other side gave way to the ocean. "We'll see. Maybe we can drive by on our way out of town on Sunday."

"Sunday," repeated Alexis. Like it was final.

Alexis pulled her arm back into the car. Claire pressed the window button, closing the windows tight. With the car quiet once more, it gave Claire a moment to clear her head.

"Saturday, Juliet has the entire day planned out for me," continued Alexis. Her voice oozing with excitement. "She arranged for us to hang out with all my friends at the usual places we love. It's going to be awesome."

"And where might that be?" asked Claire, grateful for a change in subject.

Alexis scoffed. "You know, bowling alley, pier, yogurt shop, the caves I love."

"Did you need me to drive you around? I don't mind one bit," said Claire.

Saturday, Claire needed something to make herself scarce. Kelly and Stephen were nice enough to let them stay at their house for free this weekend, but they certainly didn't need her hanging around their house the entire time. Claire promised she'd be busy the entire weekend, and only needed a place to crash at night.

"No," said Alexis firmly. "Juliet's taken care of it. You only need to drop me off at her house in the morning. Her mom will bring me by late in the evening." She glanced up from her phone, tilting her head toward her. "We can visit Mom's grave on Sunday. The gas station too. I'll make time for it."

"Then it's settled." Claire reached out, cranking up the radio. The soothing sounds of Adele blasted back at them. Claire sang loudly along with the music, hoping to forget about whatever hard parts she might have to face during the weekend.

"I still don't understand why you are so obsessed with Adele." Alexis rolled her eyes. "She's only *okay*."

Claire laughed. "Oh honey, sit back while I educate you on how completely awesome Adele is."

Shifting around in her seat, Alexis crossed her arms. "Fine," she gave her a pointed look. "Go ahead, I'm ready."

Then Claire and Alexis held a healthy debate on singers the entire rest of the way to Pismo. By the time she took the exit, Claire managed to push away her anxiety for the weekend. But as David's office came into view, her heart picked up to a steady staccato. Palms clammy, sweat smattered across her forehead, pouring down her back.

Pulling into the parking lot, Claire forced herself to sound cheerful and upbeat when she said, "We're here." She parked the car, turning off the ignition. Glancing at the clock on the dashboard, she continued, "We even managed to get here right on time."

Alexis unlocked her seatbelt. "I can't wait to tell David about my new dance studio."

"He might be busy with other patients." Claire unbuckled her seatbelt too. Opening the visor mirror, she double checked her appearance in the small mirror. She hated how much she cared. "I wouldn't get your hopes up if he can't talk to you for a long time."

"He'll have time," replied Alexis. "He told me he made sure we were his last appointment of the day."

Perfect. Claire gritted her teeth. With a shaky hand, she dug out her lip gloss from her purse.

Alexis opened her car door. Shifting, she gazed over at Claire reapplying her lip gloss in the visor mirror. "Don't worry, you look gorgeous as always. He'll totally regret ending things with you."

Claire stopped mid swipe, turning to eye Alexis. "I'm not worried about that." But even she knew how ridiculous she sounded. Here she was reapplying her lip gloss and smoothing out her hair. "My lips were chapped so I figured lip gloss would do the trick."

Alexis laughed, climbing out. "Liar." Shaking her head, she closed the car door.

Wandering across the parking lot, Alexis entered the office. With a huff, Claire slammed the visor mirror shut and tossed her lip gloss back into her purse. What did her sister know? Nothing. Getting out of the car, Claire remembered to straighten her back and pull back her shoulders.

A chime on the door announced her arrival. Sarah glanced over from her seat at the reception desk. Brightly, Sarah smiled. "You've made it. Our last appointment of the day, and only one more appointment for Ms. Alexis."

Sarah's smile was contagious, making her anxiety slowly wither away. Claire crossed the room toward Sarah.

"Yes," Claire stopped in front of the reception desk. "Alexis has been reminding me constantly." Readjusting her purse strap, Claire asked, "Should I schedule her last appointment right now?"

Sarah moved herself closer to her desk, wiggling her mouse, the schedule popped up on the screen. "Yes, let's see what we have available. Dr. Clark knows I need to leave as soon as I checked you two in." Then Sarah paused, grinning she added, "I have a big date tonight." Her eyes sparkled with anticipation.

Claire smiled. "Good luck. I hope you have a fantastic time."

"Thanks, he's something special," replied Sarah. "I'm excited." Then she waved it off.

The conversation went back to scheduling Alexis's final appointment. Once on the calendar for four weeks from then, on another Friday afternoon, Sarah left, leaving Claire in the empty waiting room.

Awkwardly, Claire took a seat, grabbing a magazine off the stack on the coffee table. Legs bobbing back and forth, she forced herself to read an article on how to look ten years younger. *If only*, she scoffed. Halfway through reading the long explanation of skin care regimens, a shuffling of footsteps into the waiting room interrupted her attention. She snapped her head in the direction of the sound. Alexis appeared. And then there David was in all his rugged, perfectly handsome glory.

With wobbly knees, Claire stood, tossing the magazine down on the coffee table. "Are you done already?" asked Claire. The words came out shaky and overly high.

Alexis beamed. "Yep," Alexis glanced over at David. "David says next time I come I get to have them taken off." She did a little dancing jig.

Claire couldn't help but chuckle, helping to release the pent-up tension in between her shoulder blades. "I'm glad you're so thrilled. I've already made the follow up appointment to get your braces off, are you ready to go?" She skillfully avoided eye contact with David, knowing a look from him would make her stomach do all sorts of weird things.

"Yes." Alexis stepped toward her. "Can you drop me off at Juliet's?"

Taking a few steps toward the door, Claire said, "I thought you were meeting up with her tomorrow and spending the entire day together. I thought we had tonight together."

David strode in front of them, opening the door. He held it open for them.

Alexis stopped on the threshold. "I'm meeting her tomorrow too, but Juliet said she's free tonight as well. I know you have nothing important planned." With pleading eyes, Alexis dragged her feet, and continued, "I only have this weekend to hang out with my friends. You must let me go. Please."

Claire shook her head, passing through the door.

Skillfully, she avoided locking eyes with David. "I understand." Digging into her purse, Claire located her keys and pressed the unlock button. "I'll drop you off at Juliet's house."

In her naïve state, Claire had thought they'd go eat something down by the pier then maybe take a walk along the beach together. But then she remembered she was Alexis's sister, not her friend. Alexis was a teenager, who wanted to spend every possible minute with the friends she missed.

Smiling, Alexis replied, "You're the best." Alexis ran ahead across the parking lot toward the car.

"Don't you know it!" shouted Claire toward Alexis. "I want that in writing!"

Opening the car door, Alexis slid inside and shut the door. Shifting a bit, Claire's gaze flickered to David.

David grinned, shoving his hands into his pockets. "I take it you and Alexis are getting along better."

Claire shrugged, trying her best to act undeterred in his presence. "I guess when you give someone exactly what they want, then it's easy to get along."

Chuckling, David replied, "True."

Being there with David, exchanging their familiar banter, made her remember how much Claire enjoyed his company. Claire lingered longer than needed.

After a few beats of silence, Claire cleared her throat. She couldn't stall any longer. "I—I should go." She pulled out her sunglasses and put them on.

"Do you have any big plans for the weekend?" asked David.

Fidgeting with her purse, Claire hiked it back on her shoulder. "Apparently not anymore," Claire gestured toward her car. Then sped on, not wanting to appear desperate. "But

I've plenty to keep me occupied. I've a few loose ends to tie up with Mom's estate."

"My parents told me you're staying at their house," replied David.

Swiping her hair over her shoulder, Claire said, "Yes. I'm very grateful. It took the worry of how I was going to pay for a hotel off my list." She studied him, wondering what he thought of the entire situation.

"My parents are good people," David glanced toward the car with Alexis in the passenger seat. "I'm glad they could help you both."

Everything clicked into place. This whole thing was about helping Alexis. Claire took a step away from him, widening the gap. "Thanks again. We'll see you in a month for her last appointment." She walked briskly toward her car without glancing back.

A commotion in her chest made her ultra-aware of what she couldn't hide. With shaky hands, Claire reached for the car door handle. The quicker she left, the less of a fool she'd be.

"Wait!" called out David.

Her heart skipped a beat. Claire let go of the car door handle, shifting to face him.

Jogging across the parking lot, David stopped in front of her. Out of breath, his words sputtered out, "I was going to walk to Splash Café tonight to get clam chowder for dinner. I thought I'd take some to my parents too. Would you like to join me?"

Her gaze skidded across his face, and Claire remembered the feeling of his stubble under her thumb, the intoxicating scent of his cologne, how being with him made the loneliness disappear. Claire still wanted him. *Don't even think about it. Say no. This isn't smart and you know it. You are going back to Los Angeles. No need to go back heartbroken, again.*

If only she would listen to herself.

With a small shrug, Claire shyly smiled. "Sure, why not."

David grinned brightly, making her middle pool with warmth. "Wonderful. I'll meet you at the pier in an hour."

Opening the door, Claire gave a small wave. "See you in an hour." Then she climbed in and shut the door.

Through the rear-view mirror, she watched as David made his way back across the parking lot and went into his office. Claire started the car, pulling out of the parking lot.

Mockingly, Alexis repeated, "See you in an hour."

Claire whipped her face toward her sister, wide eyed. When she didn't say anything right away, Alexis cackled.

"Oh dear..." Alexis wagged a finger at her. "I knew it. You're right back on track."

"On track for what?" asked Claire.

"For you and David to realize you belong together." Alexis turned her attention back to her phone. Her fingers tapped rapidly, and she didn't look up when she added, "David's going to realize he's falling completely in love with you."

"Nobody's falling in love." Claire continued through town. "We're only going to get something to eat. If you don't remember you ditched me for an evening with your friends."

"Whoops. Sorry about that," replied Alexis. "But you can't blame me. I need to stay connected with my friends especially if we move back by Christmas."

"We're not moving back!" Claire practically screamed.

Then Alexis burst out laughing. "Oh boy, you're in trouble." She laughed so hard; tears ran down her cheeks. She swiped at the corners of her eyes with the back of her sleeve. "I love seeing you like this—frazzled."

Gripping the steering wheel tighter, Claire saw her knuckles turning white. "I'm not frazzled. I'm chill as a cucumber."

Still laughing, Alexis said, "Please don't ever say chill as a cucumber again."

Claire rolled her eyes, but the tension in her shoulders disappeared.

"I'm sorry," said Alexis. "I like teasing you. Because you're easy to tease. I know it isn't funny, but you and David were distracting me from remembering things…" Her voice faded off, and she stared out the passenger side window.

Claire slowed the car down, not wanting to arrive at Juliet's house before Alexis divulged everything. Instead, Claire made a right turn, taking the longer way along the ocean.

Flipping the music playing from the radio off, Claire asked, "What things?"

Alexis exhaled. "Things like how being here makes me think of Mom at every turn." Alexis kept her gaze out the passenger side window. Claire didn't interrupt but waited for her to finish. "Sometimes I wonder if this ache in my chest will ever go away. Or how I'll ever find a way to forgive the person who did this to her—to us."

Her words pushed out every ounce of oxygen left in Claire's chest. Pulling the car to the side of the road, Claire put the car in park. Moisture tickled the corners of her eyes, Claire glanced up, blinking rapidly. Wringing her hands together, Claire tried to find the words to make everything okay. But then she knew no words would ever heal the broken parts in each of them.

"It was an accident." Claire voice came out almost in a whisper. Shifting, Claire reached out and gripped Alexis's shoulder. "The guy had a heart attack and died too."

Alexis swiped at the tears running rampant down her cheeks, seeping into her sweatshirt. "I…" Her voice cracked. "I'm still so angry Mom was taken from us." Alexis cried into her palmed hands.

Claire wrapped her arms around Alexis bringing her closer. Alexis cried some more on her shoulder.

Once Alexis's chest stopped heaving, Claire loosened their embrace a tad. "I think someday it'll get easier." She stared out the windshield, wondering what easier even meant. "I mean I pray every day for it to get better. Someday in the future, I don't know when, but we'll be able to talk about Mom without this debilitating pain in our chests. And someday you'll find a way to forgive too."

"I don't think it's possible for me." Alexis broke their embrace, swiping at her eyes with the back of her wrist. Opening the glovebox, Alexis dug out the travel pack of tissues. Pulling a tissue out of the package, she blew her nose. Tightly, Alexis grasped the tissue into a ball. "I'm so angry. I don't think I can ever stop being this mad."

Claire leaned back in her seat, gripping the steering wheel with one hand. She didn't have an answer, at least not one which quickly resolved everything. "I think it's possible." She exhaled. "I must trust someday with God's help, I can find a way to be free from this level of pain. I hold out hope, and it's hope that keeps me hanging on and moving forward."

Alexis sat rigidly in her seat, staring out her passenger side window. Silence permeated the car. Claire turned back on the ignition, pulling back onto the road. The familiar streets of her childhood passed by in a blur. If she didn't make the next right, Claire would be too late to avoid the gas station where it happened. She hesitated, wondering if it was too much too soon, but it had been over five months. Accelerating the car, Claire passed her last possible exit route before the gas station.

"Wait," said Alexis, peering over at Claire then back out the passenger window. "You're not turning…" Her voice trailed off.

Her heartbeat tripled its speed, making sweat form on her

brow. "It was your idea," replied Claire. "You're pushing me to do hard things."

Alexis slouched. "I know…" She clasped and unclasped her hands in her lap. "I thought I was ready, now I'm not so sure."

A drip of moisture ran down her back as the gas station came into full view on the right. With shaky hands, Claire drove past the gas station without stopping.

A hand flew to Alexis's chest, her breathing labored. But Alexis didn't say anything more. The light up ahead turned red, and Claire brought the car to a stop.

From the rear-view mirror, she saw the edge of the gas station. Slowly, thump by thump her heart rate returned to normal, making her stronger with each beat. "Sunday, we'll stop and go inside the convenience store."

Alexis peered over her shoulder, out the back window, taking in the remaining view of the gas station. "Okay. Sunday. I'll be ready then," stated Alexis.

"Me too," replied Claire. "Me too."

CHAPTER EIGHTEEN

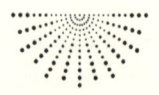

Waiting in his parked car, David spotted Claire walking down the sidewalk leading to the pier. Though it was early evening, with it being summer the sun was still high in the sky. The sunlight cast a heavenly glow, radiating off Claire's hair. David reminded himself to breathe as he stared in awe of her casual everyday beauty. A gentle breeze made her hair whip around her shoulders, and David watched as she attempted to tame the loose fly aways. After she arrived at their agreed-upon meeting spot at the opening of the pier, Claire settled onto one of the benches which faced out to the water.

She was early. And he was too. Claire was only here for the weekend, and come Sunday, she'd be gone and he would once again be alone. How could he already miss her, and she wasn't even gone yet? Restless, David climbed out of the car, locking the door behind him. He strode across the parking lot while his insides did somersaults. Then as he approached, Claire twisted on the bench, landing her glance on him. He nearly froze in place as their eyes locked, making him feel perfectly intoxicated. *You're toast. Admit it.*

With wobbly legs, he waved at her, reminding himself to smile. "Claire." He took the remaining steps to meet her. "You beat me here," said David.

Running her hands back and forth over her thighs, Claire smiled, making the corners of her eyes crinkle. "I did." David wondered if she was cold or as nervous as him.

Sitting down on the bench next to her, David forced himself to stare out at the vast ocean and not at Claire. He thought again how he loved Pismo, loved the ocean, and its ability to bathe his body in its calming balm. It was the most relaxed he felt in months.

Claire said, "I arrived early on purpose." Her gaze held steady on the water.

Resting his arm on the back of the bench, Claire relaxed against the seat, only slightly brushing his arm. A fire raged in his gut. If David only moved his arm a few inches, he could fully wrap his arm around her shoulders. His body ached to be close to her again, but he had forfeited that right, so he didn't move his arm. Forcing his hand into a fist, David tapped it unconsciously on top of the back of the bench.

"And why did you want to arrive early?" David asked, shifting his gaze from the ocean to her, allowing himself to bask in her beauty. "I—I mean if you don't mind sharing."

Turning a tad, Claire moved closer. "I wanted a few minutes to think..." Her voice trailed off, and she propped one leg over her other knee. Exhaling, Claire paused.

They were an inch from touching, and the distance was driving David batty. Finally, with a furrowed brow, Claire asked, "Do you think it's possible to truly forgive someone?"

Without hesitation, David replied, "Absolutely."

Claire glanced down at her hands then flipped her hair over her shoulder. The strands of her hair tickled his arm. "Alexis and I are trying to move on, to forgive." Her voice faded away with the waves of the tide. Gazing out at the water, she continued, "It's a tall order, to forgive. Always easier said than done, but I've always believed forgiveness is more for yourself than for anyone else."

"I agree." David ached to pull her close, but he swallowed the thought away and continued, "But if anyone can forgive, it's you."

Claire's back stiffened. "I don't know about that." Gnawing on her bottom lip, she hesitated then asked, "Do you ever think you'll forgive your ex-wife?"

The question knocked the wind right out of him. David didn't see the conversation going in this direction. They were talking about her, not him. He wanted to believe he forgave his ex-wife, Lauren, and more importantly, himself. Every day he remembered how he had failed in the biggest way possible. It ate him alive, kept him from moving on, and from finding happiness with someone else.

David crossed his arms, shifting in his seat. "I thought I had."

Claire shook her head. "No, I don't think you have. But you should. You deserve to be happy too."

Was he happy? David wondered. Claire made him happy, Alexis too.

Abruptly, David stood, wanting the talk of Lauren to be over. "Should we go get some clam chowder?" He held his hand out to her to help her to her feet.

Claire placed her hand into his, standing herself. He held her hand longer than necessary. David only realized it when Claire stared down at his grip. He broke their touch. Claire folded her arms against her body.

Shifting toward Main Street, Claire didn't acknowledge his quick change of the subject. "Let's go. I'm hungry. The line is probably already around the block."

"Yep, but oh, so worth it," replied David.

They walked to Splash Café in silence, getting in line

behind the other customers wrapped around the restaurant and down the street.

Once in the line for a few minutes, Claire, leaning up against the wall of the restaurant said, "I remember the last time I came here with Mom. Alexis complained, because she didn't want clam chowder. Mom talked her into getting something else. Tacos I think." Claire's eyes misted, and she cleared her throat. "Mom had a way with Alexis. She could talk her into anything."

"And you can't?" asked David.

Claire laughed. "No way, not even a little bit." She smiled. "But you have a way with her. She likes you, and Alexis hardly likes anyone."

David leaned his back against the building too, so they were shoulder to shoulder. Finally touching, he hoped it would squelch the desire within him to draw her close. "I'm around teenagers all day with my patients. I've learned a few tricks on how to talk to them."

Shoving her hands into the front pocket of her hoodie, Claire replied, "Maybe you could teach me a few of your tricks?"

"I'd be happy to teach you what I know." The line inched forward, and they slid along the wall, moving closer to the beginning of the line. David continued, "It isn't a lot."

Claire pursed her lips together. "Come on David, don't be modest." She nudged him with her elbow. "What do you text with Alexis about? She mentioned you check up on her."

David rubbed his jaw. "Ahh…" He didn't want to reveal they mostly talked about Claire. Alexis brought her up at every turn, feeding him unnecessary intel on how to fix whatever was broken between them. "Mainly, I ask her about Los Angeles. Her dance classes. We've talked about which instructors she likes and the ones she doesn't. That sort of thing."

Taking a sidestep, Claire moved to face him, leaning a single shoulder against the wall. "What does she say about Los Angeles?" Her brow furrowed.

The line moved significantly forward, so David pushed off the wall and walked to catch up to the end of it. Claire followed him. Once they stopped again, David gulped. "Alexis doesn't like Los Angeles." Exhaling, he shoved his hands into his pockets. "But I'm not telling you anything you don't already know."

Claire exhaled, making her shoulders droop. "I know, but there's nothing I can do about it." She gazed past him, down Main Street toward the pier and ocean. "I wish I could give her everything she wants, including living here, but I can't."

"Alexis might learn to like Los Angeles," offered David. "Give her time."

With a look of defeat, Claire said, "I hope so. We'll see."

They arrived at the front of the line and ordered their clam chowder. After settling into their seats to wait for their food to arrive, David broke the lull. "I'm sorry about how I acted the night of Alexis's dance performance."

Her back stiffened, but Claire waved it off. "It was for the best. I was leaving." She didn't look at him but kept her gaze on her soda. Fiddling with her straw, Claire continued, "The inevitable was coming, and you helped to rip off the band-aid. We couldn't be together." Her gaze skidded anywhere but on him.

"Still," David leaned forward. "I wish I had found a better way."

"David," said Claire, stopping him mid-sentence. She placed a hand on top of his forearm. "Let's leave the past in the past. We can just be friends."

The words felt like a sucker punch to the gut. He gulped. "Friends," repeated David in a nauseous haze.

But is that what he was doing, right? Being friendly.

Friends? The word felt like chalk in his mouth. After spending only a few minutes with Claire again, David realized he didn't want to be her friend. David wanted to kiss her. Love her. Be with her.

They were interrupted by the food arriving at their table. A waitress set down two sourdough bread bowls filled with steaming clam chowder. His mouth watered from the sight. The smell wafting straight off the top.

Plunging her spoon into the thick white chowder, Claire pursed her lips and blew over it. Her hair nearly fell into the bowl, so she flipped it over her shoulder. She caught him staring at her. His body ignited and heat splashed his cheeks. His thoughts were a whirling and thrilling mess. Claire was beautiful. Beautiful in a way where her goodness shone from the inside. She didn't need to be constantly told, because she embodied what it meant to glow.

Gulping, David glanced down at his food. With a shaky hand, David forced himself to take a spoonful of his clam chowder, shoving it into his mouth without thinking. The liquid was boiling hot, David managed to swallow half of it. Then he coughed and sputtered, trying to get it down without burning his entire mouth.

Claire laughed. "I thought you'd been here before." She raised an eyebrow, clearly amused.

David wiped his chin clean then took a big gulp of his soda. "I—" he coughed. His taste buds were completely gone. "I—have."

Blowing on another spoonful of chowder, Claire said, "You of all people should know they serve this stuff like liquid lava."

"I know. I was a bit distracted." David plunged his spoon in again, but this time he took the time to blow lightly on his spoon.

Spoon in hand, Claire asked, "By what?"

David shifted in his seat. Unsure if the clam chowder was cool enough to eat, he timidly tested it. Confirming its cool temperature, he ate the entire bite. Once he swallowed, David said, "By you."

Her cheeks reddened, and Claire's lips formed a tight line. She didn't reply but ate another spoonful of chowder.

David tried to remember why he let her go to begin with. *She moved to Los Angeles. You flipped after seeing Lauren.* But suddenly Los Angeles didn't seem like a long distance. As for Lauren, he didn't want her to take one more thing from him.

Shifting in his seat, David filled in the gap of silence. "How is your job going? Are you happy to be back at work?"

Claire shrugged. "It's nice to be back with my patients and co-workers. The days certainly pass by faster than before, and I find the routine cathartic. It helps me forget about the past five months. I didn't have anything to distract me, and now I do."

Nodding, David took another bite of his food.

ONCE THEIR MEAL WAS COMPLETE, DAVID WALKED CLAIRE OUT to her car. Stopping in front of her car, David lingered. Heart hammering, he finally sputtered out, "Could I call and talk to you sometime?" He shoved his hands into his pockets. He rambled on, not giving her a chance to respond. "I know I already call Alexis, but I'd really enjoy talking to you too. I miss hearing your voice."

Claire reached into her purse, pulling out her keys. Fidgeting with them, she said, "I don't know…" Her voice faded away. Claire glanced out toward the pier and ocean. The sound of the waves crashing on the shore distracted her for a moment. She continued, "I don't think that's a good idea."

His gut clenched tight. "Why not?" David pressed.

Gripping the keys in one hand, Claire tapped it against her other hand. "You know why." She tilted her head to the side.

Her words gutted him. He had foolishly played with her heart. Why did he think none of his actions mattered? David lost the claim to be anything to her, but it didn't mean he couldn't try to right the course.

"Please," David pleaded. "I like talking to you. I like being your friend."

Claire scoffed, "Friend." She shook her head, taking a step toward her car. "I— I—"

"You're the one who said earlier we should be friends," said David.

Claire halted, shifting back toward him. "True." Gnawing on her bottom lip, Claire exhaled. Slowly, she said, "I did say that."

And David knew he still had a chance. The thought made him smile. "Then I'll call you," he said.

Reaching for her car door, Claire opened it and tossed her purse onto the passenger seat. "And maybe…" she planted a single finger into the middle of his chest, "I'll pick up."

Then Claire climbed into her car and drove away.

CHAPTER NINETEEN

"Are you sure about this?" Alexis gripped onto the door, shifting to face Claire. "I know it was my idea, but I'm beginning to regret suggesting it."

Hands clammy, Claire rubbed them over the top of her thighs. "We can do it." Her voice contained a tad too much enthusiasm. "We'll go in, look around, buy some snacks like we always did with Mom."

Alexis interrupted her, "But Mom isn't here." Exhaling, Alexis stared at the convenience store.

Parked in the gas station parking lot, they spent the last ten minutes getting up the courage to go inside. Anxious energy pumped nonstop through her being. Swiping at the slick layer of sweat on her brow, she willed herself to be strong. What was she trying to prove? Her strength? Because she felt nothing but small.

Claire peered through the windshield. A flood of memories came back, ones which made her ache and miss Mom all over again. She blinked rapidly, pushing the tears away. "Do you remember how Mom always bought Pringles to take to the beach?" asked Claire.

Alexis's lips twitched with the forming of a smile. "She claimed it was the perfect beach food."

"Because it came in its own protective can," replied Claire.

"You could toss it into a beach bag, and it didn't get destroyed or crushed like a normal bag of chips." Alexis swiped at her misty eyes. Then she ran a single finger across the passenger window. "She always had an answer for everything," said Alexis softly.

"She was the smartest person I ever knew," added Claire.

"I agree," said Alexis with a slow nod. "She was like a walking encyclopedia. Anything I asked her; she'd spew out random facts about it like an expert."

"She made everything seem easy." Feeling brave, Claire opened her car door. "We can do this. Let's go in, buy the snacks Mom always bought. Then we can eat them on our drive back to Los Angeles."

Alexis peered at her. "Are we still stopping by Mom's grave on the way out of Pismo?"

"Yep," Claire climbed out. "I've already bought the flowers. It's our next stop before driving home."

"Home," Alexis scoffed. She climbed out too, shutting the door behind her. "This is home, not Los Angeles."

Claire slouched, but she quickly tried to straighten her back. "But perhaps someday Los Angeles can feel like a second home."

"Unlikely," muttered Alexis.

Claire didn't know what else to say, so she said nothing. They walked in without stopping. While wandering the aisles looking for what they needed, Claire tried her hardest to keep telling Alexis stories she remembered about Mom to distract Alexis and herself. Claire didn't want to ruminate over how Mom died or the why, but instead fill the space in her mind with the beautiful memories they shared together.

After purchasing the snacks, stopping at Mom's grave, and then the long drive home back to Los Angeles, Claire was emotionally depleted. As the view of their apartment appeared in the windshield, Claire wanted nothing more than to crash face forward on her bed and sleep until morning.

Once parked, Claire and Alexis climbed out.

Unloading their luggage from the back of the trunk, Alexis grabbed her bag from Claire. "When do we go back to Pismo?" asked Alexis.

"In a month." Claire slammed the trunk shut and grabbed her roller suitcase. "I set the appointment for the week before school starts. You'll get to start at your new school with no braces. I think that's something positive to focus on."

"But that's the last time we'll go to Pismo for who knows how long," whined Alexis. She begrudgingly put on her backpack. "I will have nothing to look forward to after we go."

Walking across the parking lot toward the elevators, Claire replied, "We'll visit Pismo as much as we can."

She had no clue how often. They didn't have a place to stay, and hotel rooms were expensive in the little beach town. Maybe she could promise Alexis one visit a year? It sounded dismal even to her. Hopefully when their lives were more settled and Alexis made friends, Pismo would become less and less important.

"When?" Alexis followed behind her with her own luggage.

Arriving at the elevator, Claire hit the up button. "I can promise we'll visit once a year."

"Once a year!" Alexis shrieked. "That's not enough. I'll miss my friends too much."

Her patience was wearing thin. A low grade headache made her neck throb. "You'll make new friends here. I can't promise you more than once a year. I don't have the money." She waved a hand between them. "We don't have the money for expensive hotels, gas, and food. I am only a physical therapist. And Mom left us a mountain of unpaid bills. Remember?"

The elevator doors swung open. They shuffled inside. Alexis punched their floor button with a closed fist. "Everything is so unfair." Alexis crossed her arms, leaning against the elevator wall. "I hate it here." Her eyes narrowed into tight slits.

The elevator jolted up. Claire sucked in the air. "I thought you liked the new dance studio. You said it was challenging you, and you were improving quickly."

Alexis jutted her chin up. "I lied."

Alexis didn't speak to Claire for the rest of the elevator ride, or the walk to their apartment. Then after dumping her stuff in her room, Alexis returned to the living room and turned on the TV while Claire scrounged around in the fridge for something to put together for dinner. Locating some bread, cheese and butter, Claire decided on grilled cheese sandwiches with some canned tomato soup. When flipping the sandwiches over in the hot pan, Alexis's phone rang.

Alexis muted the TV and answered, "David," replied Alexis. Her voice was animated once more.

Claire's ear perked up. David. Flipping off the gas burner, Claire plated the sandwiches. Alexis continued to chat with David while Claire strained to hear what they were talking about. Besides the carefree laughs from Alexis, Claire couldn't decipher the conversation. Grabbing two bowls, Claire filled them with the steaming tomato soup. Taking them to the table, along with the sandwiches, Claire waved at Alexis and pointed at the table ready with food.

Alexis turned her back to Claire, covering her face with

her hand to no doubt keep Claire from listening in on their conversation. Claire shrugged and settled into her seat and began to eat. A few minutes later, Alexis walked over to the table and sat down.

Holding out her phone, Alexis said, "David wants to talk to you."

"What?" Claire wiped her face with her napkin, shifting in her seat. "Tell him I'll call him when I want to talk."

"No." Alexis shook the phone, pushing it into Claire's hand. "We both know you won't call him back. Just take it and talk to him."

Exhaling, Claire slowly took the phone from Alexis. She pointed at the food and mouthed, "Eat." Then she put the phone to her ear and said, "David, what's up?"

"I heard it was a rough day," said David with a voice as silky smooth as butter.

Running a hand over the top of her hair, Claire eyed Alexis taking slow bites of her sandwich and eavesdropping at the same time. Claire stood, placing the phone in the crook of her neck. Grabbing her dishes, she walked to the sink.

"Was that what you two were talking about?" Claire flipped on the faucet and quickly rinsed her dishes, placing them in the dishwasher.

"Partly," replied David.

Claire twirled back to the table, covering the mouthpiece, she told Alexis to eat then shower. Then Claire took her hand off the phone and walked to her bedroom. "And what was the other part about?"

"I promised Alexis I wouldn't tell," said David.

Claire plopped herself down on her bed, kicking off her shoes in the process. "What part can you tell me?"

"I can tell you Alexis said today was hard. She misses her mom, friends, and Pismo."

Claire pinched the bridge of her nose. "That makes two of us, but there isn't anything I can do about that. We've been over this."

"I know," replied David.

A long pause. Claire cleared her throat. "Was there anything else?"

"How are you doing?" asked David.

Shifting her phone from one hand to the other, Claire flipped onto her side. "Exactly how do you think I'd be doing?" Her voice cracked, and she hated how quickly David was breaking down her resolve. She knew she shouldn't be telling him anything. Claire needed to get over him, and talking to him would only do the opposite.

"Not good, I'm sorry," said David.

His words vibrated around in her brain.

With a long sigh, Claire said, "Everyone is always sorry, but they're not living my life." Claire knew she needed to stop complaining. There were plenty of people out in the world who were way worse off. But there was something soothing and calm about telling one person that everything felt hard and difficult. And David happened to be an excellent listener. "I'm barely holding it together." She blew out a long, shaky breath. "I think our visit to Pismo did more harm than good. Seeing everyone made Alexis miss everything even more, and now Alexis is walking around like she hates me and her life."

"She's upset you can only visit Pismo once a year. She doesn't think it's enough. If she knew she could visit more, then it wouldn't feel so heavy," revealed David.

With a clenched jaw, Claire shrieked, "It's all I can afford!"

"You can always stay at my place for free," offered David. "And my parents really don't mind you staying at their place either. Look, that's two practical options right there for you."

"Thanks, it's nice of you to offer. But your living situation might change. You might find a girlfriend, wife, whatever and I'm sure they wouldn't appreciate us staying there." Claire ran a finger across the top of her pillowtop duvet cover. "I don't want to promise Alexis something and not be able to deliver. It'll only make things worse between us."

"I don't plan on finding a girlfriend or wife for that matter," stated David.

"You don't know," said Claire. "You might wake up tomorrow and fall in love with someone you meet at the supermarket."

David paused so long Claire worried the connection dropped.

Pulling the phone away from her ear, Claire double checked the connection. "David are you still there?" she asked.

His voice cracked as he said, "I'm still here."

"Okay," replied Claire.

"Hang in there Claire. And Claire," his voice dangled in the air.

"Yeah," Claire rubbed her jaw.

"It'll be okay. Just remember Alexis is a teenager who lost everything. She's struggling. Cut her some slack."

Claire gripped the phone so hard it made her knuckles turn white. "I'll try to remember that." Anger bubbled up in her chest. The last thing she needed was to be reprimanded by him.

"I'll call you tomorrow," said David.

"And I might pick up," Claire snapped back.

Then she abruptly ended the call before David could reply further. She threw Alexis's phone down on top of her bed and screamed into her palmed hands.

CHAPTER TWENTY

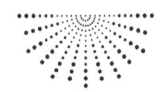

"Dr. Clark." Sarah's voice stopped David in his tracks.

He backpedaled the few steps to her reception desk. "What's up, Sarah?" David flipped through the chart in his hand, adding a few notes to the patient's chart.

Sarah shifted in her seat and waved for him to come closer. Leaning over her arm rest, Sarah glanced out at the people sitting in the lobby. Once she confirmed they weren't paying attention, she whispered, "Your ex-wife is on the phone."

His blood ran cold. David cracked his neck in both directions. "My ex-wife?" he repeated. "Why is Lauren calling?"

"I don't know." Sarah gnawed on a fingernail. "I tried to get her to tell me, but she wouldn't. Do you want me to take a message? I can tell her you're busy."

Sweat slathered his brow. He tugged at the collar of his shirt. "I—" David glanced at his watch, then out at the patients waiting in the lobby to be seen. Lauren knew he was busy during the day. He wondered why she was contacting him, but he didn't want the dread of calling her back hanging over his head forever either. "I'll take it in my office if she's willing to wait five minutes."

Sarah stared at him. "If that's what you want me to do…" Her voice trailed off. "Lauren's on line three." She shifted back and took the phone off hold, telling Lauren the instructions David gave her.

Shaking his head, David strode into the exam room and finished checking the adjustment on one of his patients. Once he approved the patient to leave, David begrudgingly walked to his office and shut the door behind him. Running a shaky hand through his hair then down his face, he forced himself to take a few deep breaths to dampen the anxiety bubbling up. After David felt his heart rate return to a somewhat normal pace, he sat at his desk and picked up the phone.

He pressed the flashing red button on line three. "Lauren," said David, forcing his voice to sound even.

"David," Lauren replied. Her voice was overly upbeat and friendly. "I was calling to check in."

"Check in!" David hissed. Then he remembered to take it down a notch and not allow Lauren to force him back into the familiar dark hole it took him so long to crawl out of. David leaned forward, leaning his elbow on his desk. "Lauren…" his voice was perfectly neutral. "Why are you calling me at work?"

"Because, I know you blocked my number," whined Lauren.

For a split-second David almost felt guilty, then he remembered he blocked her number after she played Russian roulette with his heart. Jerking him back and forth for months even though she never planned on reuniting with him.

"I did," David slowly stated.

"David, it was so good to see you a few months back," said Lauren. "I've missed you."

"Fine." David's jaw clenched. He rubbed it nearly raw. "Again, why are you calling me at work?"

Lauren exhaled, "Like I said. I've missed you."

David closed his eyes for a moment, cupping the back of his neck. This was the Lauren he remembered. One who was always looking around for someone better. She married Zach, but now she called to say she missed him. Nope. This was not happening. He refused to even entertain this entire conversation. Lauren would always be Lauren, and if anything, time taught him he deserved someone who would be faithful to him, encourage him, believe in him, not someone who yanked their love away when someone else caught their eye. Someone like... Claire. He smiled at the thought.

"Lauren," David sat up straight, regaining his confidence. "I'm going to have to stop you right there."

"Why?" asked Lauren. "Why, can't I call to tell you I've missed you, and I haven't stopped thinking about you since that night at the dance performance?"

"No, Lauren." David stood. Energy pulsated through him. "You can't call me at work. You are married to Zach. You chose him over me. Remember?" He didn't wait for her to answer. "You need to be faithful to him. We're divorced. Our relationship is in the past. I wish you and Zach nothing but the best. I hope you two are happy together. But please don't call me again."

Speaking the words out loud, settled the pit in David's stomach. He was moving on, and perhaps he was finding a way to finally forgive Lauren in the process.

"David..." Lauren pleaded. "Please..."

"Lauren..." David sat back down, leaning back in his

chair. "Go and be happy. Don't worry about me. I'm good. Happy even."

"But David…" Lauren's voice faded away.

Silence followed. David no longer cared what Lauren hoped to gain by calling him. It didn't make any difference. If anything, this conversation brought him the closure he desperately needed.

"Lauren, I wish you all the happiness in the world but don't call me again. It isn't appropriate. I'll tell Sarah to take a message if you try again," stated David with resolve.

"I— I—" stammered Lauren. When she finally continued, her voice was small and quiet, "I'm glad you're happy. Bye."

Then the line went dead. David set the phone back on the receiver and breathed a sigh of relief. In the past, a conversation with Lauren would've left him reeling for days. Today was different because David knew he didn't want Lauren. Not even close. Claire was the one he desired, and he needed to win her back.

Standing up, David wandered back to reception to find Sarah. Sarah glanced up when he approached. "Hey, everything okay?" asked Sarah.

David nodded, "I've never been better." Grabbing his next patient's chart from the stack, he flipped it open. Without looking up, he continued, "I need to win Claire back."

Sarah laughed. "I wasn't expecting you to mention Claire." She shifted, leaning a tad closer. "But I'm happy to hear you've come to your senses."

"We need to table this for now." David glanced out at the crowded waiting room. "But I'll need your help and ideas."

"I'm on it, boss." Smirking, Sarah wagged a finger at him. "Don't worry, I'll help you come up with the perfect game plan."

His entire being was lighter. "Wonderful." David smiled.

Then he announced the next patient's name. The patient stood and David ushered him back. The rest of the day flew by. His back-to-back appointments gave him little time to dwell on his conversation with Lauren.

While sterilizing his medical instruments at the end of the day, David heard Sarah approach. She leaned against the door frame leading into the storage room. "So..." Sarah said. "I've been speaking with my boyfriend on ways to help you dig yourself out of this hole you've gotten yourself into..."

Closing the door to the sanitizing machine, David pressed the start button. "Since when do you have a boyfriend?" He leaned against the counter, folding his arms.

"Since like a month ago." Waving it off, Sarah took a step into the small storage room. "But we aren't talking about me."

"I can't let you off that easily." David raised an eyebrow. "You have to at least tell me where you met him."

"Here," stated Sarah. She held her gaze steady as if challenging him to question how it. "He's a patient. He had braces as a kid, but he lost his retainer and his teeth moved. He ended up with Invisalign."

"Which patient?" asked David.

Sarah scratched her head. "Dylan," she said, shifting her weight.

David only had one adult patient named Dylan. "Dylan Mutton?" asked David.

"Yes," said Sarah.

"If I remember correctly, he works at the resort down at the far end of Pismo," replied David.

"Yes, he's the hotel manager, because his family owns the place, but, Dr. Clark." Sarah raised an eyebrow. "We aren't talking about me right now. I'm trying to tell you how to win Claire back."

Uncrossing his arms, David stood straight. "Oh right…"

"So," continued Sarah, "when does Alexis come back for her final appointment?"

"In two weeks," replied David without hesitation. He'd been secretly counting down the days until they both came back to Pismo. "I've been talking to Claire every night on the phone. That's something, right?"

Sarah beamed. "You're better off than I thought. Please continue talking to Claire every day. Make sure you ask her lots of questions about her life and then listen. Also, you need to ask her out and plan a proper date for when she's here. On the date, you confess to her how you feel about her."

Nodding, David slowly exhaled. "I think I'm in love with her."

Sarah's eyes dilated. "If that's the case, when Claire's here you need to tell her you're in love with her. After you tell her, then you can ask her to come back to Pismo to live."

The idea halted him in his tracks. David ran a hand down the length of his face. How could he ask Claire to return to Pismo? Her job was in Los Angeles. Even if he did love Claire, it didn't mean she loved him back or was anywhere near uprooting her life yet again for them to be together. His knees became wobbly as his head spun in a tizzy.

"I—I don't know," stammered David. "I can't ask her to do that. She's already told me she doesn't have the money to move back."

Sarah tsked. "Then you're going to figure out how to help her with that too."

David bit the inside of his cheek. "And what do you suggest?"

Sarah rolled her eyes. "I can't do everything for you, boss." She threw her hands down at her sides. "You're smart. You'll figure it out." Then she didn't linger and left.

David stayed in the quiet of the storage room. He wanted Claire back, but how was it feasible for them to be together? But then a brilliant idea popped into his head, and he wondered why he hadn't thought of it sooner.

CHAPTER TWENTY-ONE

EVERY DAY AFTER WORK, CLAIRE COUNTED DOWN THE MINUTES until David called. It was always in the evening before Alexis went to bed. He always spoke to Alexis first. During their conversations, it was the only time Claire saw Alexis's smile or her laugh. Alexis was miserable in Los Angeles.

Claire's days were busy and chaotic. She'd shuttle Alexis to the dance studio, race to work, spend the entire day helping clients, rush home to make Alexis and her something for dinner. By the time the evening rolled around she was zapped. Claire appreciated Mom more than ever. All those years as a single mom, Claire wondered how she made it look so easy.

So, once the dinner dishes were done, and Alexis and she settled on the couch together to watch a home renovation show, Claire looked forward to one thing--David calling. He always listened patiently, encouraging her. After their conversations ended, Claire felt reinvigorated.

A week before their final return to Pismo, Claire was talking to David on the phone. It was past eleven, and Alexis had fallen asleep an hour earlier. Claire lounged on the sofa with a blanket sprawled across her legs, and the TV muted with some PBS Masterpiece classic playing.

"Claire..." David said after a slight pause in their conversation.

"David..." Claire replied.

"Are you free next Friday night? Or will you be hanging out with Alexis?" asked David.

Her lips quivered. Maybe David enjoyed their reconnection as much as she did. Clearing her throat, Claire tried her best to sound casual. "Alexis will be with friends from the minute she gets her braces off on Friday. Basically, she'll only be with me to sleep. She's been talking nonstop about who she plans on showing her teeth off to first."

David chuckled. "I'm sure she'll do exactly that." Another pause. "Anyways..." His voice trailed off. Claire's heartbeat rang in her ears. Finally, after what seemed like an eternity, David continued, "I wanted to see if you'd be interested in going on a date with me."

A shot of adrenaline zinged down Claire's back. Sweat smeared across her forehead. She tried her best to sound flirty when she said, "I could maybe pencil you in."

"Could you pencil me in for six?" asked David. "I— I thought I could take you to Grover Beach. They let you drive right onto the sand, and we could eat and roast marshmallows in a fire pit."

"I love Grover Beach." Claire sighed as a wave of childhood memories ran through her.

"I love it too, but does that work?" asked David.

"It sure does." Claire smiled to herself. "It's a date."

∽

CLAIRE CRANKED UP THE MUSIC IN THE CAR, LETTING THE smooth, silky sounds filter out the inch gap of her lowered windows. Smiling, in a sing song voice, Claire said, "Only one more hour of having those braces on."

Glancing over from her cell phone, Alexis laughed. "I thought I was the only one counting it down."

"Nope," replied Claire. Her fingers tapped to the beat of the music. "I'm excited to see your beautiful smile too."

"I think you're more excited to see David again." Alexis gave her a once over then wagged a finger up and down the length of her body. "I noticed you have on a brand-new dress, and I know you spent ten extra minutes this morning applying your make up."

Claire tugged on the top of her floral summer dress. "This old thing." Jutting up her chin, she continued, "I have no idea what you are talking about."

"If by old, you mean, yanking off the tags before you put it on a few hours ago," replied Alexis. "Then I guess that's old."

Claire chuckled. "You caught me." She glanced ahead at the upcoming curve in the road. One side was the picture-perfect Pacific Ocean, the other side was carved out mountain.

"I applaud you at your effort." Alexis peered over at her. "I think you look fantastic. It's going to make David regret ever letting you go."

"I— I—" Claire stammered. Then she shrugged. "I don't know what's going to happen this weekend. Probably nothing life altering, but I'd be lying if I said I wasn't the tad bit optimistic."

"I'm hopeful too." Alexis changed the station on the radio. "Like I've been saying all along…" She kept flipping through the stations, clearly looking for a song she found more appealing. "You and David need to get married so we can move back to Pismo Beach."

Her back straightened and shoulders stiffened, Claire

stammered, "I— I didn't say anything about us getting married." Claire fanned her flushed face. "I don't want you to get your hopes up. David and I have only been talking to each other. Nothing more. This could be dragged out for years. Or he could meet someone in Pismo tomorrow and then this…" she threw up an exaggerated hand. "Whatever it is will fizzle out."

"But he asked you out on a date. And you look like a knockout." Alexis finally landed on a radio station she liked and leaned her head back against the headrest. "By the end of this weekend everything will be figured out. I know it. I can feel it in my bones." Casually, Alexis stared out the passenger side window, tapping along to the steady beat of the song's melody.

Claire heard no sound, only the thundering of her heart. Her and David getting married? Ridiculous. "No…" Claire started to argue.

"Shh." Alexis reached out, placing a calming hand on her shoulder. "No more talking, this is my favorite song." Then Alexis reached forward and cranked up the volume.

With a sigh, Claire listened to the song, ending the conversation. An hour later, they pulled into the parking lot of David's orthodontist office.

Alexis unbuckled her seatbelt. "Juliet and her mom are coming at the end of my appointment to see the big reveal of me without braces," said Alexis with enthusiasm. "Then they're taking me to meet up with some other friends. I only plan on being at the house to sleep. So, you are free to hang out nonstop with David. I'll be busy."

"You know I don't mind having you, right?" asked Claire.

As difficult as it was navigating the emotional rollercoaster of a teenager, Claire was grateful to have Alexis. If it had been only her, alone during these past months, it would've been unbearable. In a way, the two sisters were saving each other.

"I know." Alexis opened her door and climbed out. "But let's be honest we both could use a break from one another."

"Alexis," said Claire. "I don't feel that way…" Her words were cut off from the slamming of the car door.

Claire watched as Alexis skipped across the parking lot to the front door and entered.

Flipping down the visor, Claire opened the mirror. With a finger, she smoothed out the outline of her lips and swiped under her eyes. Once satisfied with her appearance, Claire closed it.

Palms sweaty, Claire climbed out of her car and strode across the parking lot. Before she entered David's office, she took a few deep breaths to calm the swimming sensation in her gut. *Chill out. It's only David.* Once her emotions were in check, Claire opened the door, entering the lobby.

Sarah gazed up from her computer as the door chimed. "Claire," she said with a smile. With a thumb, Sarah motioned toward the exam room. "Alexis has already gone back. She'll be done in about an hour if you needed to run an errand."

Claire strode further into the waiting room, stopping in front of Sarah's reception desk. "I'll wait." She wrung her hands together, peering into the exam room. Claire couldn't see David or Alexis from her obstructed view. "I don't have anywhere else I need to be."

"Okie dokie," Sarah stood, pushing in her chair. "Dr. Clark said I could leave once you arrived, since Alexis is the last patient for the day."

Adjusting the strap of her purse over her shoulder, Claire shuffled her feet. "Oh, okay."

A knot formed in her stomach, and Claire reminded herself to breathe. It had been a month since she'd laid eyes on David, and she wondered if she'd still feel a connection between them. Or worse, she wondered if David wouldn't feel anything at all.

Sarah's overly animated voice broke her train of thought. "Dr. Clark hasn't stopped talking about you both coming." Walking around the desk, Sarah moved closer. After she glanced into the exam room, Sarah leaned in closer and whispered, "And I know he's excited for your date tonight."

Her cheeks burned. Claire gulped. "I'm looking forward to it too."

Patting her on the shoulder, Sarah said, "Yes, so no need to be nervous. David has a great night planned." Sarah walked the remaining steps to the door. Motioning with her head, she continued, "Why don't you go on back. You can watch as he removes Alexis' braces. There isn't anyone else here. He made sure of that. I'm sure he'll enjoy seeing you earlier rather than later."

Then Sarah made her exit.

Clasping and unclasping her grip around her purse, Claire finally mustered up the courage to move, passing through the threshold into the exam room. David was hunched over Alexis with his hands in her mouth. As she shuffled closer, David paused, peering up at her. The air crackled with palpable intensity. Seconds ticked by like infinity. Heat smothered her cheeks. It was there, and she couldn't quench it, even if she tried.

"David…" Claire finally managed. Using the back of her wrist, Claire swiped at the moisture gathering on her forehead. Throat dry, Claire swallowed, trying to find her voice once more. "It's good to see you again."

David gulped, making his Adam's apple bob up and down. Dropping the instrument in his hands, he bent down to pick it up. "Claire, I'm glad you're here." Another pause, then David shook the instrument in his hand. "I need to get a new one. Please take a seat." He motioned toward an empty chair on the other side of Alexis.

With legs like jelly, Claire walked to the available seat, lowering herself into it. David hadn't moved yet but remained frozen with the dropped instrument in his hand. She leaned closer to Alexis, examining her teeth. "Alexis, it looks like David is halfway done." She patted her on the shoulder.

"I can't wait to see what my teeth look like," replied Alexis.

"Yes. Yes." David stammered. Suddenly, he moved to leave. "Yes, halfway there. Let me go get a new one of these." He quickly left, leaving Alexis and Claire alone.

Alexis burst out laughing. "You two." She rolled her eyes. "It's very entertaining to watch you guys interact with one another. I thought David's eyes were going to fall out when he saw you."

Claire shifted in her seat. "Enough," she hissed. "He'll be back any second. And I don't want him to hear you talking."

Alexis adjusted her position in her chair. "Of course," Alexis scoffed. "Why would you want David to know how you feel about him?"

Pursing her lips together, Claire wondered how to respond. Luckily, they were interrupted when David returned with a clean instrument. After settling back into his seat, David continued to remove Alexis's braces. Claire forced herself to not stare at David but focus her attention on Alexis's teeth.

Once the last brace was removed, David announced, "Are you ready to see your new smile?" He pushed a button to lower the exam chair back to its normal height.

Nodding, Alexis waited until the chair stopped moving then she swung her legs over the side. "I'm ready. Let me see them."

"You look fantastic." David grabbed a mirror off the side table. He held it out to her. "Take a look at your new beautiful smile."

Taking the mirror from David, Alexis caught her new look for the first time and gasped. "My teeth look beautiful." A wide smile spread across her face, making her sparkle. Alexis moved her face in different directions to take in her smile at all different angles. "I knew my teeth would look good, but I can't believe what a drastic change it is. I love it."

Claire clapped her hands together. "Alexis, I'm so happy for you. I love your new smile. You look beautiful."

Handing the mirror back to David, Alexis said, "David, you're a miracle worker."

Placing the mirror on the side table, David chuckled. "I'm not a miracle worker only a simple orthodontist."

The door chimed, and a few seconds later Juliet and her mom wandered into the exam room. Alexis leaped from her chair, pointing at her new perfectly straight teeth. Both oohed and awed at the sight. Once the appropriate amount of praise was given, they moved to leave with Alexis in tow.

Before leaving, Alexis ran back and gave David a big, huge hug. "Thanks, David. I'm so happy," she said.

David hugged her back. "It was my pleasure. Now go and have a great time with your friends. You can eat all the candy you want. Your dentist can deal with the consequences."

Claire walked Alexis and Juliet out to the parking lot, double checking with Juliet's mom about the girls' plans for the weekend and confirming what time Juliet's mom would drop her off later that evening. They drove off, and Claire wandered back inside to the empty office. The lights in the exam room were off. Claire peeked into the next few rooms looking for David.

A room past the bathroom had the lights on, Claire called out down the long hallway, "David, are you back there?"

She waited for a reply.

A second later, David emerged from a side door. He flipped off one of the hallway lights as he strode toward her. Claire froze in place, locking eyes with him. Gulping, her palms began to sweat, and her insides turned on themselves.

Managing to find her voice, Claire said, "There you are." Without thinking, she fluffed her hair unnecessarily.

Without breaking eye contact, David closed the gap between them. Clearing his throat, David replied, "Here I am." He reached, giving her hand a small squeeze before letting go. "Did Alexis get off okay?"

Claire nodded. "She's off and ready to live her best life."

"How about you?" David tilted his head, studying her. "Are you ready to go? Or did you want to swing by my parents' house first to drop off your stuff?"

Catching a whiff of David's manly scent, Claire nearly stumbled forward while she said, "I don't care. Either way."

Wrapping an arm around her shoulders, David's steady strength settled her. "If you don't care, let's head out. I don't want to miss the sunset. I have everything packed and loaded into my truck. Sarah helped me get everything ready," said David.

"Sounds perfect," said Claire.

Then David kissed her on the temple, breaking their physical barrier even more. "I can't wait."

The words rang in her ears, nearly making her pool into a puddle on the floor. Leading Claire out of his office, David locked up and then took her hand as they walked across the parking lot to his truck.

His skin against hers sent a zing down her back. And BOOM. Claire knew she was in love.

CHAPTER TWENTY-TWO

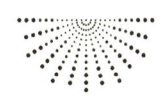

At the stoplight, David tugged at his collar. Stealing a glance at Claire, he asked, "Is the temperature, okay? Or should I adjust it?"

Before she responded, David reached out and cranked up the air conditioning. Was it just him? Or was his truck suddenly a thousand degrees? His brow slick with sweat, he swiped it with the back of his hand. He turned his attention back to the stoplight.

"I'm fine." Claire shifted in her seat, leaning closer to him. "But I don't mind you blasting the AC."

"Sorry, I tend to run a little warm." David pushed up the sleeves of his shirt. "It's one of my many glaringly obvious flaws."

Claire laughed. "Flaws?" She squeezed his forearm. "You're such a liar. I happen to think you're terrific, nonexistent flaws and all." She smiled warmly.

"I think my ex-wife would beg to differ," replied David.

"Lauren's an idiot," Claire stated flatly.

David chuckled, easing the tension in his neck and

shoulders. His nostrils flared from a whiff of her perfume. "Enough about Lauren. Did the drive go okay? Any traffic?"

Claire replied, "There was a little traffic getting out of the city, but overall, not too bad." She gazed out the passenger side window, staring at the view of the ocean peeking out between the homes. "I don't know when we'll make the trip again. Once Alexis starts school, we won't have the time or money to keep coming down here."

His gut clenched tight. "I'd love to see you and Alexis whenever you manage to come up," said David.

David wished he knew a better response. He wanted to scream *Pick me! Pick Pismo!* But how could he ask that of her? What did he have to offer her? *You could marry her.* He let the idea settle.

Shifting in her seat, Claire paused. She opened her mouth to speak, but then quickly shut it. Finally, after a long pause, she said, "I'm sure we would enjoy seeing you too."

Grover Beach came into view. David pulled into the parking lot then followed behind the few other cars making their entrance onto the packed sand. He drove slowly, but the truck bounced up and down on the uneven sand.

Claire gripped onto his arm. Her fingernails nearly piercing his skin. "Are you sure this is safe?" She glanced at him. "Have you done this before? Or is your truck going to get stuck? I can't dig us out. I don't have the upper body strength."

The sand smoothed out some, making the ride less bumpy. Claire released her hand.

"We'll be fine." He pointed at the long string of cars in front of him. "If I follow behind them, I promise, we won't get stuck. We're almost there." He glanced to his right, taking in the spectacular view of the ocean. With a contented sigh, he continued, "Just in time for the sunset."

Pushing some loose strands out of her eyes, Claire tucked them behind her ears. "My favorite part of the day."

David smiled. "I'm glad to hear it."

After finding a spot along the beach, secluded enough, David parked the truck. They both climbed out, wandering to the back of his truck. Together they unloaded the wood, food, chairs, and blankets.

After setting up the chairs, David said, "Do you want to sit for a while?" He rested his hands on the back of one of the camp chairs. "I can get the fire started while you relax."

Holding up her hands, Claire replied, "You won't hear me argue." She plunked herself down in one of the chairs. "I know I would be zero help to you anyways."

David gave her shoulder a squeeze, before walking back to the bed of the truck. After he grabbed his shovel, he started digging a pit deep enough in the sand to start a fire. In the midst of digging, David felt Claire's gaze on him. When David couldn't take it anymore, he glanced over at Claire, locking eyes with her. His heartbeat increased to a fast staccato beat. Fumbling around and nearly dropping his shovel, David wiped his hands on his pants and went back to digging. Once the pit was completed, he tossed in some firewood and managed to start the fire.

"I'm very impressed," said Claire, interrupting the silence. "I had no idea how skilled you were in wilderness survival. Were you a boy scout?"

Laughing, David shook his head. "No, I was never a boy scout." He strode over, sitting down in the chair next to her. Their arms brushed each other on the armrests. "I did do a backpacking trip with some buddies after college, through the Pacific Northwest. We stopped at a few national parks."

"Amazing," Claire pulled the blanket on her lap over her shoulders. "I've only walked the trails around here. Nothing that comes close to something that adventurous."

Straightening his shoulders, David found his confidence. "I'd love to go hiking around here with you. I'd take a day hiking with you over a trip with a bunch of knuckle head guys, any day of the week."

Her cheeks tinged pink. Claire's gaze skidded from him to the ocean. "I'd love to go hiking with you sometime."

David wrapped his arm around her shoulders, giving them a squeeze. "Let's go tomorrow. I know the perfect place to take you."

"Sure," Claire snuggled closer to him, making her body heat seep into his skin. "No time like the present."

The blanket fell from Claire's shoulders, and David helped readjust it over her body again. Both stared out at the ocean and the sky, breathing in the bliss of the evening. Slowly, the last little bit of sunlight stretched across the water, rippling streaks of red and orange in the sky. David glanced from the ocean to Claire. She looked beautiful, more beautiful than he remembered.

Reaching out, David traced the outline of her jaw with a single finger. "I want to spend every spare moment with you. Even if we only have this weekend. There's nowhere else I'd rather be than with you."

Claire sucked in the air, holding his gaze. Pausing, she swallowed and moistened her lips. "I'm glad we have today, and I'm here with you."

David's gaze flickered between her eyes and lips then back again. He remembered the feeling of holding her close, of kissing her, and David wondered how or why he had ever let her go. Why hadn't he chased after her car when she drove away? How had he been so wrong about so many things? Like believing love wasn't worth the risk a second time.

"Claire," whispered David. He moved his hand to cup her

neck. "I've…" He struggled to find the words to express the feelings trapped inside of him.

"Go on." Her words tickled his neck, sending goosebumps down his back. "What is it?"

"I have been thinking all day, every day, about kissing you," said David. The words came out far too shaky and less smooth than he anticipated. With a trembling hand, he ran his thumb across her temple. "You make me…"

Shifting closer, Claire placed a flat palm against his chest. "I make you what?"

Lungs compressing, David said, "You make me believe in forgiveness—in love."

Claire gulped. Her voice came out almost as a whisper. "You make me believe in those things too."

David edged his body toward hers, leaning as far as possible over his armrest, waiting for confirmation to continue. Slowly, Claire tilted her head to the side and lightly grazed his lips. Body ignited. His nostrils flared with the sweet tantalizing aroma radiating off her hair. He deepened their kiss, wanting to taste more of her. Her lips danced with his own. Twisting and twirling. His head spun and chest nearly exploded. David reveled in the tender feeling of being kissed by the one he wanted to be his.

For a moment, he slowed their kiss, taking the time to memorize the gentle glide of her jaw, the outline of her cheeks, and the warmth of her skin. David wanted Claire to be the only person he ever kissed again. Wrapping his arm around her shoulders, David tugged her body as close as possible with the restriction of their chairs. Kissing her long enough, he lost track of time.

Finally, David forced his lips away from hers. Resting his forehead against her, he waited for his breathing to even out. Breath by breath, his heartrate returned to a normal pace.

Once back in control, David kissed Claire on the temple, tugging her body to his side. His hands glided down the length of her long silky hair in hypnotic strokes. For a long time, without speaking, they held one another.

On the horizon, the setting sun dipped even lower, and they said goodbye to another spectacular day. Darkness enveloped them as a half-moon replaced the sun. They sat under a blanket of stars. A log in the sand pit crackled, spitting out a few sparks.

Claire jolted and her hand flew to her heart. "That scared me," said Claire.

"You're so cute." David kissed her on the temple, unwrapping his arms from around her. "I hope you know that." A blush splashed her cheeks, and she smiled.

Standing, David crouched next to the fire pit, grabbing another log from the pile. Poking the smoldering logs with the tip of the wood in his hand, he rearranged the logs to prevent them from burning out too quickly. Once satisfied with the position of the logs, he tossed a fresh piece of wood on top.

Pivoting back around, David peered over at Claire. "Are you hungry?"

Smoothing out the top of her head, Claire shifted in her seat and shrugged. "Sure, I could eat."

David paused, wishing he could confess his true feelings for her. If was bold and more confident, he would've blurted out he loved her. Like really loved her. Part of him dreamed she would repeat the words back. He shook it off. What would a confession do if they continued to live in two different places? The thought depressed him as there appeared to be no path forward.

Gulping, David moved toward the cooler of food. "I'm hungry too," he managed. Opening the cooler, he unpacked the food. "I have some sandwiches and pasta salad. We can eat the sandwiches first."

"Sounds wonderful," said Claire. She flashed a smile revealing her sparklingly white teeth. "I don't care what we eat. I didn't have to cook, so I'm happy."

Her being glowed with the reflection of the bonfire. David was stilted by her beauty but reminded himself of what he was doing. Digging out the food, he carried the sandwiches along with two sodas over. Sitting back down, he held a sandwich and soda out for her. Claire took both.

Putting her drink in the cup holder of her chair, Claire peeled back the paper on the sandwich. Licking some avocado from the wrapper that smeared on her finger, Claire then took a bite. After chewing she said, "David."

"Uh..." David shifted, looking for a place to set his soda. He spotted the cup holder in the armrest of his chair and placed it inside. He then found her gaze, waiting for her to continue.

"I—" Claire shook her head, "I— Never mind." Taking another bite of her sandwich, Claire chewed and swallowed. Her eyes glazed over as she stared at the smoldering logs in the fire.

David nibbled on his own sandwich, though he didn't taste anything. Their shared kiss ran rampant through his mind, replaced by the reality Claire was leaving again on Sunday. His heart sank. He already missed her, and she wasn't even gone yet. He knew this time she'd be gone for good. David didn't want to ruin the evening. Claire knew of their situation, and even with the cards stacked against them, Claire stayed.

Once they finished their food, David took Claire's hand, interlocking their fingers. Soothing waves pushed back at the doubts whirling around in his head. On this blissful night, with twinkling stars up in the sky smattered against the dark night, David held everything that mattered. With the darkness, a chilly wind whipped between them, but with their bodies close to one another and crackling fire, they stayed warm.

Neither spoke about tomorrow or what the future held. Instead, they sat enjoying the quiet serenity of the beach, together, until the last log burned out.

CHAPTER TWENTY-THREE

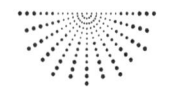

Claire didn't sleep a wink in David's old childhood bedroom. Tattered posters of rock bands from his youth covered the walls. His dresser was lined with trophies from soccer, basketball, and football teams. She tried to imagine David twenty years younger.

As the sunlight pushed through the slit in the curtains, Claire glanced across the room at the other twin bed which held a still sleeping Alexis. Grateful for a few more minutes to think, Claire snuggled deeper under her covers. Flipping to her side, images of the night before played on repeat in her mind. Claire had gone off and fallen in love with David, again.

Smiling, she remembered their stolen glances, heart-stopping looks, and a kiss to top everything. Maybe they could work? Maybe David loved her too? And if they loved each other, somehow, they'd find a way to be together. Right?

But who was she kidding? David might still be tainted about commitment. Her reality crashed down on her, making her mind a muddled mess. A cold sweat broke out across her forehead and chest. Claire flipped the covers off her body to cool herself down. The rapid movement woke Alexis.

Alexis stirred in bed. Flipping to her side, Alexis rubbed her eyes. "Good morning," said Alexis, half yawning. "What time is it?" She sat up, swinging her legs over the side.

Claire mirrored her movements. "Only eight. But I've been awake for a while." Swiping the sweat off her brow with her wrist, Claire avoided eye contact with Alexis.

Alexis studied her, raising an eyebrow. "Everything okay?" she asked.

Waving it off, Claire stood, stretching. "You bet, never better."

"Liar." Alexis stood too, smoothing the covers back in place. For a teenager, Alexis was surprisingly neat and tidy. "Did last night go the way you wanted?" She tilted her head to the side and studied Claire.

After David dropped her off, Claire sat out on the porch overlooking the ocean. The view was spectacular and calming. By the time Claire finally sneaked into their bedroom, Alexis was already sleeping soundly.

"Unfortunately, it went too well." Claire gnawed on her bottom lip, running a hand over the top of her hair. "Why did I have to go off and fall for a guy who lives a four-hour drive away from me?"

Alexis squealed. Jumping up and down, she clapped her hands together. "Finally! I thought you'd drag this thing out for another year. I'm thrilled you've come to your senses."

With a hand on her hip, Claire replied, "But we live in Los Angeles." Claire threw her hands down at her sides. "We can't be together, because we live so far apart."

"Boo hoo. Nonsense." Alexis strode to her suitcase, grabbing out an outfit to change into. "By Sunday, you'll have it figured out."

"I'm glad one of us is confident." Claire shook her head

and strode to her own suitcase. "I'm sure not," she muttered under her breath. Then Claire spun back toward Alexis. "When will Juliet be here?"

"Any minute," Alexis changed out of her pajamas, pulling on some jeans and a T-shirt. "Her mom is taking us to Old West Cinnamon Rolls for breakfast." Just then Alexis's phone vibrated. Alexis swiped it off her bed stand, checking the message. "They're here." She shoved her phone into her pocket and slipped her feet into her sandals. "Don't wait up for me." Then Alexis rushed out the door.

Flopping backwards onto the bed, Claire covered her eyes with her arm. She didn't know what time David planned on coming by the house. They'd only established he'd come by in the morning to take her for a hike. After lounging for a few minutes, Claire regathered her clothes and went to shower. After showering and changing, Claire left the bedroom and wandered down the hallway. She heard chattering in the kitchen. Though she couldn't make out what they said, David's distinct voice alerted her.

Smiling, Claire strode further down the hallway. Then hearing her name, Claire halted in place. Her heartbeat picked up speed, making her temples pulsate. Leaning up against the wall, Claire knew she shouldn't eavesdrop on the conversation, but something told her to stop.

Kelly continued, "So, what are you going to do now? Claire and Alexis are going back to Los Angeles tomorrow."

"I don't need to be reminded." David's voice oozed annoyance. "I'm going to see how today goes. Then I'll decide."

Decide what? Claire gulped. Sweat dripped down her back. Was this some type of test? And if she didn't pass then what?

"This is such a big decision." Kelly hissed in a half

whisper, "I don't know— I just hope it goes the way you want."

"Don't you know I'm aware of what might happen? Don't you think I've weighed it all out? I've done nothing but think about it," replied David. "Enough, I don't want to discuss this anymore."

"Okay," replied Kelly with sigh loud enough for Claire to hear out in the hallway. "I'll pray for the best to happen."

Claire exhaled. Her stomach twisted into a knot. She wanted to burst into the kitchen and declare she heard everything so they might as well tell her what it meant. But she didn't. Instead, Claire dug into the pocket of her shorts and dabbed her lips with some lip gloss. Once applied, she squared her shoulders and walked the remaining distance into the kitchen.

In an overly animated voice, Claire announced loudly, "Good Morning," as she crossed the threshold into the kitchen.

Kelly jumped, skirting her glance. "Good morning, Claire. I hope you slept well." She picked up a rag and wiped an invisible spot on the counter.

With a plastered smile, Claire replied, "I did, thank you."

Halving the distance between them, David said, "It's good to see you." He pulled her tight in an embrace, and Claire hugged him back.

Half nauseous, Claire broke their embrace. To appear casual, she leaned against the kitchen counter. She forced herself to shake off what she overheard. "Have you been here long?" asked Claire.

Joining her, David leaned against the counter next to her, crossing his ankles. "Nah, not too long. I was here to greet Alexis before she rushed off."

"Yes, we won't see her for the rest of the day," added Claire. She then noticed Stephen reading the morning paper at the breakfast table. "Good morning, Stephen. I didn't see you over there."

Stephen said hello but then went back to reading the newspaper, flipping to the next page. Claire didn't even know people still did that.

Shuffling her feet, Claire met Kelly's gaze. "Thanks again for letting us stay here for the weekend." She gripped the counter on both sides of her. "Alexis and I are very grateful."

Tossing the rag in her hand into the kitchen sink, Kelly waved it off. "Anytime. It's no trouble at all." Warmth oozed back into her voice. "We're happy to help." She washed and dried her hands then shifted back around. A silence lingered. "Can I make you two something for breakfast?"

"No." Claire glanced quickly at David. "David promised to take me to breakfast before we go on a hike."

Wrapping an arm around her waist, David brought her hip to hip. Then kissed her on the temple. "I sure did."

Kelly's gaze scrutinized the two of them together. Claire hoped she saw how perfect they were for each other.

With a nod, Kelly replied, "That's nice. I hope you have a nice time together." She walked and sat down next to Stephen at the breakfast table.

Releasing his embrace, David pushed off from the counter. "Should we go? Are you ready?"

"Yes, let's go," replied Claire.

They said goodbye to Kelly and Stephen. Claire followed David out of the house and to his truck.

Once both settled into the cab, Claire asked, "Are your parents okay with us dating?"

With keys in the ignition, David paused turning to face her, "Yes, why?"

Shrugging, Claire shook her head, peering out the passenger window. "I don't know..." She gnawed on the inside of her cheek. "I overheard you guys talking, but I didn't know if it was a good thing or bad. Do your parents disapprove of me?"

Shaking his head, David replied, "No disapproval." He rubbed his jaw. "They just don't want to see me get hurt, but it has nothing to do with you. I promise. My parents love you and Alexis."

She wished his words put her at ease, but they didn't. Wringing her hands together, Claire stared down at them, avoiding eye contact. "What about you?" Her voice cracked. Emotion bubbled up inside of her. Claire wished she wasn't this unsure of where they stood. "How do you feel?"

Leaning closer, David reached out and tilted her chin toward him. "Come on." His gaze bore into hers, making her temples pulsate. "I'm totally hooked on you." His voice was soft and velvety. "I thought I made that abundantly clear last night."

Her middle pooled with warmth. Claire couldn't help but smile. "You did. I guess I'm just in my head."

"That makes two of us." David dropped his hand and started the car. Double checking the road, David pulled out. "Have you ever eaten the breakfast sandwiches from Beachin' Biscuits?"

Claire shook her head. "No, but you had me at biscuit."

Grinning, David drove the rest of the way to the restaurant. It was only a few blocks away. After they ate, David drove them to the Meadow Butterfly Trail. The spot was popular.

Once they walked for a few minutes, holding hands along the trail, Claire revealed, "I used to come here all the time as a child. It makes me miss Mom so much my heart aches."

David gave her hand a squeeze. "I'm sorry." He paused, running a hand through his hair with his free hand. "I wish I had more to offer than that. Are you okay with staying? Or should we turn back?"

Hooking her hands around the crook of his elbow, Claire replied, "I'm good to stay." The first of the tall sand dunes peeked out at the end of the trail. "I'll always miss Mom, but I'd rather remember the good memories than not think about her."

"Makes sense," David said. "I loved this place as a child too. My dad and I would fly kites here. It always seemed to be windy enough."

"I flew kites here too." Claire smiled as more memories flooded her mind. "It's the perfect place. Because in the fall it's too cold to get into the water, but you can still enjoy being at the beach."

"Exactly," replied David.

Approaching the first big sand dune, Claire released her grip. "I'll race you until we reach the water." She didn't wait for a reply.

Sprinting, Claire dug deep going up and over multiple sand dunes. Soon David sped out in front of her, taking the lead. Claire nearly tumbled forward as she ran down the next dune, but she managed to regain her balance. Eventually, the sand flattened out, giving way to the ocean. The water glistened. David arrived a few seconds before Claire, stopping right at the edge of the harder wet packed sand. Claire came up beside him.

Leaning over, Claire placed her hands on her knees as she regained her breath. "You beat me." Her chest heaved, slowly her heartbeat leveled out. She plopped herself down on the sand, removing her shoes. "But you have longer legs than me."

David sat down next to her, removing his shoes too. "True which is why I was okay with your head start."

Claire laughed. "I cheated, and I still lost."

Leaning back on both of his flattened palms, David crossed his ankles. "Let's call it a draw." He smiled.

Nudging him with her elbow, Claire said, "Fine. I can live with that." A zing raced down her spine as David stared back at her. Finally, she forced herself to look out at the ocean and not at him. She took in the beauty of the beach, the blue of the sky, and the sound of the seagulls. All. Of. It. She wanted to remember this perfect day forever. "I'm going to miss this view..." Her voice trailed off and sadness overtook her.

Claire feared their future together. She'd go back to Los Angeles, and most likely her and David would slowly fizzle out. Again. A long pause, both sat staring out at the ocean. Claire brought her knees close to her chest, cradling them with her arms. If she looked over at David, she knew she'd cry. Why did she have to find love now? When there wasn't a way for them to be together.

David sat up, brushing the sand off his hands, he wrapped an arm around her shoulders. "What if you didn't have to miss it?" His voice shook.

Claire whipped her head toward him, finding his glance. "What—what do you mean?" She searched his face for understanding.

"What if you moved back?" asked David.

Immediately, Claire shook her head. "How? I can't afford it here. My job is in Los Angeles. I mean I could look for a job in San Luis Obispo, but I still don't think I could afford it. The jobs out here at these small hospitals don't pay as much."

"I understand that." David reached out, pushing her hair over her shoulder. His hand lingered, cupping the back of her neck. "I've been thinking about your situation a lot. What if we got married? You and Alexis could move in with me. It's small, but it does have two bedrooms. We could look for a bigger place once you both are settled."

Shaking her head, Claire straightened her legs and ran a hand through her hair. "I— I—" She glanced down. "I don't know what to say."

"Say yes," replied David.

Claire paused, closing her eyes for a moment. "This is what Kelly knew about." Gnawing on her lip, Claire forced herself to listen to the rhythmic crashing of the waves against the shore. "Marriage... I mean have you even begun to think how life-altering that would be for you. Because it's not just me. I'll always have Alexis. She must be included."

"I've done nothing but think this thing through. I love you more than anything, but I love Alexis too. Together we could be a family." David tilted her chin, meeting her eyes. His gaze bore into hers, making her gulp. "I admit, I was scared. I pushed you away. I was afraid of failing at everything a second time. But not anymore." His voice cracked. "I want to marry you. I want us to be together."

Claire blinked rapidly. "I— I— don't know what to say."

David replied, "Say you love me too. Say you want what I want too."

"You know I love you." Claire repeated the words slowly. She exhaled, making her chest heave. "I've loved you since the day you came to my house and helped me with that garage sale."

Grinning, David replied, "Your words mean the world to me." He kissed her quickly on the lips then continued, "I'll say it again until I'm blue in the face. I love you. Please, pick me. Pick Pismo. Marry me, and I promise I'll do whatever it takes to make this thing between us work. I've already failed once at marriage, and I don't plan on repeating it. Because I've fallen completely, can't live without you, head over heels, in love with you. And I'm sorry I let you go. I wish I hadn't. I regret it, but I don't want to live any longer with regrets. We both know life is short. There are no guarantees we will have tomorrow. So let's not wait."

"Do you mean it?" Her voice shook as her hand found his chest. Her fingertips picked up the steady beat of his heart.

"You'd love me enough to marry me… even with me having Alexis?"

"Yes," David kissed her then pushed her unruly hair over her shoulder. "I love you. I love Alexis. So please, marry me."

"Then, yes," Claire grinned. "I'll marry you."

His breath tickled her neck. "Then I'll be the luckiest guy ever."

With a fist of his cotton tee, Claire yanked his body closer to hers. "Let's call it a tie for who's the luckiest."

Then under the brilliant blue sky, with the sounds of the waves crashing beside them, Claire skated her lips across his, an addicting thrill skimmed down her spine. Remembering all over again, the feeling of his stubble against her cheek, the glide of his jaw under her thumb, and the support of his arm around her waist.

His cologne made her nostrils flare and body buzz. Soon, she was transported elsewhere to a place where the worries of the future withered away, and it was only her and David. Everything before had brought them to this place, holding one another, kissing, in Pismo, like it was the first and last time all wrapped up into one. There they were, together, picking each other, picking Pismo.

EPILOGUE

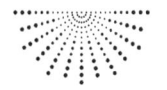

Loading the stroller into the back of the minivan, Claire asked, "Did you grab the diaper bag?"

Holding up the bag, David came around the van. "I have it right here." He placed it in the back of the van.

Claire kissed him lightly on the lips. "Thanks." She wiped her sweaty brow with the back of her wrist. "I knew you had it. I'm just nervous. I don't want to be late."

David squeezed her shoulders. "I know but you don't need to be. Alexis is going to crush her graduation speech."

Her chest heaved. "Let's hope so. Alexis wouldn't even let me read it. I really don't know how this is going to go."

A cry from inside the van interrupted them. Claire closed the back of the van.

David went around to the side, opening the sliding door. "And what's wrong missy?" He leaned over their eighteen-month-old daughter, twisting around in her car seat. Her face was bright red. Slowly, he stroked the side of her face, and with the other hand he searched for her pacifier. After locating it on the floor of the van, he held it up. "Is this what you wanted?" David popped the pacifier back into the baby's mouth.

Claire almost lunged for the pacifier. "That was on the floor." Her eyes widened.

Their daughter stopped crying and happily sucked on the pacifier. David handed her a favorite stuffed animal. She gripped it in the crook of her elbow. He hit the button to close the sliding door.

"It's fine." David tugged Claire close, wrapping his arm around her waist. He kissed her lightly on the lips. "She'll live. You look beautiful by the way."

Claire laughed, waving a finger at him. "Don't you change the subject."

"What?" David kissed her temple. "Can't a husband tell his wife how gorgeous she looks."

"I hate how much this is working." Claire smirked and put a hand on her hip. "But we'll talk about dirty pacifiers later."

"Sure thing." David opened her door, gesturing to her to climb in. "Later. We don't want to be late to Alexis's graduation. It's not every day your sister will be graduating from high school."

After settling in her seat, Claire wrung her hands together. "I can't believe this day has finally come. Thank you for your help in raising her. I couldn't have done it without you."

"Yes, you could have. But I appreciate your gratitude." David shut the door and walked around to his side, climbing in.

So many changes in the last five years, David never realized how much his life would improve for the better. His heart filled with gratitude as he started the van, pulling onto the road. He reached for Claire's hand, interlocking their fingers. Even after all this time, he still yearned to feel her close.

"I can't believe Alexis is attending Boston Conservatory at Berklee in the fall." Claire glanced over at him. He could feel her studying him. "It's way on the other side of the country."

David gave her hand a squeeze. "I know it'll be hard at first, and you'll miss Alexis. But she worked so hard to get in, I'm happy for her. We'll visit. I've always wanted to go to Boston in the fall to see the leaves change."

"I know you're right." Claire exhaled. "Everything is changing, sometimes I wish everything could stay the same."

"But where's the fun in that?" asked David.

For a while, they remained silent. As David turned into the high school parking lot, Claire interrupted the quiet. "I guess it's good Alexis is going off to college. It'll give us some more room for…" Her voice faded away.

Putting the van into park, David turned off the ignition and shifted to face Claire. "Give us more room for what?"

"For the baby," said Claire.

David glanced over his shoulder at his now sleeping daughter. "She already has her own room." He raised an eyebrow.

Claire shook her head. "Not that baby. For the new one."

His jaw dropped. "Claire, are you telling me we're having another baby?"

Gripping his knee, Claire nodded her head. "Yes. I'm pregnant!"

"I— I—" David stammered. Finally, he smiled and kissed Claire on the lips. "I'm so happy. How did I end up being this lucky?"

Claire nudged him with her elbow. "Because you were smart enough to marry me." She unbuckled her seatbelt. "But don't tell Alexis. I don't want anything to ruin her big day."

"It's our little secret." David leaned in and kissed her. "I love you."

"I love you, too," replied Claire.

MEET THE AUTHOR

Emi Hilton is a California native who was born at March Air Force Base, to an Officer in the US Army Combat Engineer Battalion father and an English Professor mother. Emi followed in her mother's footsteps and graduated from Brigham Young University in English. While in college, she took a year and a half break from her studies to serve as a full-time missionary for her church in the Canary Islands. Emi writes sweet contemporary romance novels. Her debut novel, Memories in Morro Bay, was nominated for a Whitney Award. When Emi isn't writing, she enjoys training for marathons, fishing off local piers with her husband and three sons, or visiting her other love, Spain.

OTHER TITLES FROM

5 PRINCE PUBLISHING

5 Prince Publishing
Picking Pismo *Emi Hilton*
Spring Showers *Sarah Dressler*
Secret Admirer Pact *Bernadette Marie*
The Taste of Treachery *Emily Bybee*
The Publicity Stunt *Bernadette Marie*
A Trace of Romance *Ann Swann*
Descendants of Atlantis *Courtney Davis*
Holiday Rebound *Emily Bybee*
Rewriting Christmas *S.E. Reichert & Kerrie Flanagan*
Butterfly Kisses *Courtney Davis*
Leaving Cloverton *Emi Hilton*
Beach Rose Path *Barbara Matteson*
Aristotle's Wolves *Courtney Davis*
Christmas Cove *Sarah Dressler*
A Twist of Hate *T.E. Lorenzo*
Composing Laney *S.E. Reichert*
Firewall *Jessica Mehring*
Vampires of Atlantis *Courtney Davis*

Milton Keynes UK
Ingram Content Group UK Ltd.
UKHW022156040824
446478UK00001B/42

9 781631 123825